His Offer Was On The Table...
...And His Face Was Just Inches From Hers.

She bit her lower lip. A part of her wanted Conner to talk her into this deal. That way, she wouldn't have to accept all the blame for the fallout.

"Tell me something that will make it worth my while. Sweeten the pot for me," Nichole said.

"I want you."

Those bald words sent a shiver down her spine. She wanted him, too, but she wanted him to want her enough to not make it a business deal.

She licked her lips, and he tracked the movement with his eyes. His pupils dilated right before he brushed his lips over hers. Just that touch sent a pulse of desire through her entire body.

She turned her head to the side. "I want you, too, but I'm not going to give in to physical desire."

"That sounds like a challenge." He flashed a wicked smile. "You should know I never lose."

Dear Reader,

This book was just an absolute dream to write. From the moment Nichole Reynolds appeared on the page, Conner couldn't keep his eyes or his hands off her. I was trying to create something a little different with these characters. I wanted them to be smart and sassy with lots of zingers flying back and forth, but I also needed them to be real people with real problems to deal with.

Conner was almost easy once I decided that he'd be single, because the one man from whom he should have learned how to be a husband and father—his own—had betrayed him. That set in stone the kind of man that Conner was. He secretly longs for something he can never have.

Nichole just wants the story of a lifetime at first, but then as she gets to know Conner she wants so much more. She really hopes that she can heal that injured part of him, never realizing that his idea of whole might be very different from hers.

I hope you enjoy reading this book as much as I enjoyed writing it.

Katherine

KATHERINE GARBERA

A CASE OF KISS AND TELL

HARLEQUIN®

entertain, enrich, inspire™

Recycling programs
for this product may
not exist in your area.

ISBN-13: 978-0-373-73190-9

A CASE OF KISS AND TELL

www.Harlequin.com

Printed in U.S.A.

Books by Katherine Garbera

Harlequin Desire

KATHERINE GARBERA

is a *USA TODAY* bestselling author of more than forty books, who has always believed in happy endings. She lives in England with her husband, children and their pampered pet, Godiva. Visit Katherine on the web at www.katherinegarbera.com, or catch up with her on Facebook and Twitter.

This book is dedicated to Rob, Courtney and Lucas.
I love you guys.

Acknowledgments:

There are many people to thank for their help and support during the writing of this book. First of all, my husband for giving me the freedom to just write—there truly aren't words to thank you for that. Also to my kids for just making me laugh when I was stuck on the plot and couldn't figure out where to go. And last, to my editor, Charles Griemsman, for being a great sounding board for ideas and of course for his deft editing.

One

Conner Macafee was used to reporters snooping around his family. His great-uncle had been a confidant of John F. Kennedy, and Conner's own family were considered American royalty in politics and business. Of course, they had more than their share of scandals as well, which had always kept the press interested in them.

But Nichole Reynolds, the society reporter for the national newspaper *America Today,* was going about it in an entirely new way. She'd crashed his family's Fourth of July party in Bridgehampton and was doing her best to fit in, but so far she'd done little but stick out. She'd tried to blend by faking an ennui with the dignitaries and A-list celebs who were in attendance. But Conner couldn't help but notice her gushing more than once to the model and polo star Palmer Cassini.

Conner had gone to school with Palmer and knew him to be a fun-loving partier. He was an intense athlete, but also a hell of a fun guy, and Conner counted Palmer as one of his closest friends. But Palmer didn't hold his interest the way the redheaded reporter did.

He knew why Nichole was here. He'd turned down numerous interview requests from her and her bosses. He understood that she was a friend of Willow Stead, the producer of *Sexy & Single,* the reality television show that featured his company, Matchmakers, Inc. With the TV show under way, Nichole intended to write a series of articles on the matchmaking service his grandmother had founded. But he didn't trust reporters and never talked to them. That's why he had a marketing manager, Zak Levy, who was handling all the promotion and press releases. Conner had been very careful to keep out of the spotlight.

"Who is she, Conner?" his mother, Ruthann Macafee, asked, coming up next to him.

"Who, Mother?" he asked, pulling his gaze away from Nichole. He assured himself that keeping an eye on the reporter was the only thing that interested him. Not her lush red hair, which flowed in waves past her shoulders, or the stunning white sheath dress she wore. But he knew that he was lying to himself. He wanted her and if he'd had any idea how potent the attraction would be, he would have granted her an interview at his office weeks ago.

"The woman you keep staring at? I don't recognize her so I suspect she doesn't run in our circles," she said. His mother was sixty-five but looked at least fifteen years younger, thanks to her active lifestyle. She played in a tennis league and ran a charity. She'd never been the type of woman to sit at home, and Conner admired her for it. Even when a plane crash had taken his father's life and revealed a scandal that would have broken many women, she'd carried on in that quiet strong way of hers.

"Nichole Reynolds—reporter," Conner said.

"Oh, dear. I wonder why she's here." He heard a hint of fear in his mother's voice. She didn't like reporters, and with good reason. He wrapped his arm around her shoulders in a quick hug.

"That reality TV show I'm doing…she wants to interview me."

"Truly? Are you going to do it? It's so gauche to talk about your private life." Conner bit back a smile at his mother's attitude. To say she was old school was a major understatement.

"I'm well aware of that," he said, leaning down to kiss his mother on the forehead. "I think I'd better get rid of her before she makes any problems for us."

"Good idea. Do you want me to ask Darren to escort her out? How did she even get in here?"

"The head of security doesn't need to be bothered with this," Conner said. He'd been handling women like Nichole since he'd turned fourteen. "She probably came as a plus one."

"Next year I'm going to make sure that the invitations are better vetted," his mother said. "I don't want her kind getting in here."

"Whose kind?" his sister, Jane, asked, joining them.

Jane was a posh and trendy woman who had her own cooking and lifestyle show on TV. She didn't shy away from the media the way Conner and his mother did, but then Jane had been sheltered from most of the fallout from their father's infidelity.

"A reporter."

"Scourge of the earth," Jane said, winking at him. "Where is she? I'll go take care of her."

His sister was a troublemaker, and Conner knew the only way to deal with her and their mother was to end this conversation. "I'm handling it."

"Which one is she?" Janey asked.

"The redhead," his mom said.

"Oh, I see why you want to 'handle' her. Go for it, big bro," Jane said.

"Mom, I think you should have disciplined Janey a lot more when we were younger. She's a complete brat."

"She's perfect," their mom said as Jane stuck her tongue out at Conner.

He shook his head and walked away from both women. He worked his way through the well-heeled party crowd, picking up a firecracker mojito—Janey's creation—from a uniformed waiter on his way to Nichole and Palmer.

She glanced up as he approached, and Conner saw the guilty look in her eyes a moment before she masked it with a brazen smile.

"Conner Macafee," she said, with a little too much enthusiasm. "Just the man I've been wanting to see."

"Nichole Reynolds," he said, matching her energy. "Just the woman I don't remember inviting."

"With women there is always some sort of intrigue," Palmer said.

"Indeed," Conner agreed. "Are you enjoying yourself?"

"I always do," Palmer said.

Nichole looped her arm through Conner's and led him away from Palmer. "If I waited for an invitation from you, I'd never have the chance to talk to you in person."

"That's because I don't do interviews." Conner's father had been very involved in politics. Even after he'd left office, he'd been in a high-profile business that had demanded lots of press and reporters having access to his life. As a teenager Conner had been photographed and interviewed by every society magazine. He'd hated living in a fishbowl and had vowed never to allow it to happen again once he was an adult. Something he'd been very successful at, even though he lived a jet-set life and had a reputation as something of a player, he didn't give interviews and was seldom, if ever, caught by the paparazzi.

"I think you're reacting negatively to someone in the past," she said, dropping her arm from his once they were far from the crowd. "I promise it will be painless."

"Maybe I like pain," he said, primarily to bait her but also because there were times when pain was the only reminder he had that he was alive.

She narrowed her gaze as she stared at him; he knew she was trying to guess if he was telling the truth. "So how about answering a few questions?"

"No, ma'am."

"I'll do anything to get this interview, Conner."

The hint of determination in her tone intrigued him. It had been a long time since anyone had been so dogged to get something from him.

"Anything?"

"Yes," she said. "I'm known as the girl-who-gets-her-story and you're making me look bad at work."

"We can't have that now, can we?" he asked, stepping closer into her personal space and letting his hands fall lightly on her shoulders. She was tall for a woman—probably five-eight—but she only came to his chest and he liked the feeling of power he had looking down at her.

"You do know I don't give interviews," he said.

"But this is different. You're doing a television show."

"Not me, my company. There's a very big difference," he said.

"Your dad didn't see it that way. He practically lived on the pages of the *Post*."

And that was precisely why Conner wouldn't. "I'm not my dad. And the answer is still no."

"Please," she said, tipping her head back and pouting up at him.

Her luscious red lips made him want to groan out loud. He felt a zing of lust shoot straight through him.

"I might do it, but the price will be high," he said, knowing he'd never sit for an interview with her. But he wanted her and didn't see why he couldn't indulge the fantasy a bit.

"Name it," she said.

He lifted a strand of her hair and wrapped it around his forefinger. She held her breath as a blush spread over her neck and cheeks. Her creamy skin with the light dusting of freckles was smooth under the fingers of his other hand.

He wanted her.

But he knew he'd never have her. He couldn't be with a woman he couldn't trust, and at the end of the day her loyalties would always be with her newspaper. But he wasn't about to let her go without stealing at least a kiss from her. He suspected the shock of what he was going to say would drive her away and maybe even cost him that kiss he wanted so badly. But that was his intention. Self-preservation won out over lust...well, sort of.

"Be my mistress for a month and I'll answer all your questions," he said.

Nichole stared up into the bluest eyes she'd ever seen and tried to make sense of what he'd just said. She'd never imagined she'd be so turned on by someone so...well, conservative. She would have to call him that. To be honest, he was so far out of her league, she knew he must be toying with her.

She was used to doing whatever it took to get a story but this was...risqué and daring and she wanted to say yes. But ethics made her back down. She suspected he'd said that to push her away and that made her mad.

"A month?" she asked. "What kind of secrets are you hiding, Mr. Macafee? I had only planned on asking you about Matchmakers, Inc. But for that kind of price, I'd have to have full access to every part of you."

She knew he wouldn't negotiate with her. Why would he? She'd read the papers back when his father died. She knew the scandalous stories of the second family that Old Jed Macafee had kept hidden and she remembered seeing the photos of Conner and his sister, Jane, as they'd been caught leaving the country on a private Learjet owned by a Greek billionaire. There had been something so sad about the once-press-friendly teenagers suddenly donning dark glasses and refusing to look at the cameras.

Conner was never going to let her interview him. She'd known it was a long shot from the beginning, but she'd gone after it anyway. Her dad always said you had to break a lot of eggs to make an omelet.

"No, you wouldn't," he said. "If you agree to this, I will specify the parameters and if you break one of the rules outlined for you, then you leave and never bother me again."

She shook her head. "If I agree, then we will hammer out an arrangement that works for both of us. Why would you even suggest this?"

"Because I know you are going to say no," he said with the confidence of a man who knew he held all the cards. "Though I would really like to kiss you."

She knew the offer of an interview had been too good to be true. She'd never be able to be someone's mistress. Her mother would have a cow for one thing. She raised all her daughters to be strong and independent. But that didn't mean that Nichole didn't long to feel Conner's arms around her.

"One kiss, one question?" she suggested.

He arched an eyebrow at her. "And that would be enough for you?"

"Is one kiss really going to be enough for you?" she countered. She had never felt instant lust for a man before. Well a man in real life. There was no denying that the first time she'd seen Daniel Craig as James Bond she'd been in instant lust. But this was real. Conner was touching her and she didn't want him to stop touching her.

"No," he admitted.

"Good. Then we keep the kiss-question ratio?"

He shook his head. "One kiss is all I want. More than that and you'd have to agree to being my mistress."

His mistress. That sounded oddly exciting to her as she'd always secretly wanted to be Gigi and have Louis Jourdan take a look at her and decide he wanted her. But could she do it?

"I want to do a series of interviews about dating and the way that our society is dominated by online dating sites and services like Matchmakers, Inc. I hadn't planned on asking you anything personal, Conner," she said.

"You wouldn't have asked me if I ever used those services?" he asked.

She shrugged. "Okay, I would probably have asked you some personal questions, too. I'm a good reporter."

She was dying to know if his father's secret family was the reason why he was still single. And she knew that if she got this story from him, she could name her own price and sell it to the highest bidder. But the price was high. Could she still look at herself in the morning if she agreed to this kind of arrangement?

Newspapers paid for interviews all the time, but paying with her body...well, it didn't feel right to her. Could she string Conner along? Make him think she'd sleep with him and sort of give him enough kisses to get what she needed without going through with it?

Ugh! She had no idea. Especially since the spark of lust that had ignited from the first moment she'd seen him was now growing inside her.

Conner was asking her for something she'd never given any other man—control over her body. But he was offering her something he'd never given any other woman—entrée into his very private and secluded life.

"I thought so. What will it be, Nichole? Do you want to come with me and be my mistress or should I signal one of the security staff and have you escorted from the property?"

She tipped her head to the side, weighing the matter carefully. Of course she should say no. There was no other answer that made any sense. But being sensible wasn't at the forefront of her mind just now.

She was intrigued. Turning away, she led him to a bench surrounded by high hedges so they had some privacy.

His hands were on her shoulders, the waves of his body heat engulfed her and the scent of his one-of-a-kind after-shave enticed her. She wanted, at the very least, one kiss.

"I can't decide until I've had one kiss," she said. She'd always been a gambler who wasn't afraid to take a chance and maybe get the big payoff. A kiss shouldn't be that big a deal. But there was something in Conner Macafee's eyes that made her believe it was.

"Why?"

"So I know exactly what I'm bargaining for. Sexual chemistry doesn't always add up."

He stroked one hand down her bare arm until he reached her waist. Wrapping his hand around her, he drew her closer until they were pressed against each other. His other hand slid deeper into the hair at the back of her neck. He positioned her so she was off balance and she had to grab on to him. She held him at his waist and looked up again into those blue eyes of his.

He lowered his head slowly, watching her the entire time, and she licked her lips, which felt dry. But Conner didn't move any faster. He had thick lashes that were as dark as his black hair. They were pretty, she thought, but then everything about this man seemed to be pleasing to her.

She felt the brush of his breath over her mouth a second before his lips touched hers. His were moist and hard and perfect. The caress of their mouths was light and made her lips tingle. He angled his head and then she felt the tip of his tongue slide over her lips and into her mouth.

He rubbed his tongue over hers and she forgot to breathe as the tingling from her lips spread down her neck and chest. Everywhere he touched her became a hot spot of intense feeling and she leaned more firmly into him. She pushed her tongue against his and tasted the inside of his mouth.

He pulled back, but continued to hold her. She knew that walking away from Conner Macafee was the only sensible thing to do. But her body was aching, her breasts felt full and she wanted to rub them against his firm chest. His eyes were narrowed as he studied her and she saw a hint of indecision in those eyes.

That hint was enough to convince her that Conner was as thrown by their embrace as she was. She held on to him, lifting her head and rubbing her lips over his one more time before stepping back.

"So, is it question time?"

"Yes. And that counts as a question," he said.

Damn. She should have realized that playing games with

him was going to be a challenge and winning wouldn't be that easy.

"Let's talk," she said. "I didn't realize you'd be so tricky."

"Not tonight," Conner said. "I have to get back to the party."

She wasn't about to let him walk away...not like this. She stopped him with her hand on his arm. He half turned toward her and she stepped in front of him and put her hands on either side of his face and kissed him for all she was worth.

His hands went to her waist, holding her to him as his mouth fell to hers. This kiss was brazen and bold, earthy and sensual. It tore her apart at the moorings, leaving her nothing to hold on to except Conner. And she clung to him.

She was shivering as he lifted his head and came back for nibbling kisses before he gently disengaged from her.

"So yes to being my mistress?" he asked. His tone was arrogant, but she knew he had every right to feel confident. She'd just thrown herself at him. "Not so fast. I have a question for you and no cheating like last time."

"Why do you want to ask me another question?" he asked.

"I need to be sure the information you're giving me is worth the price I'm paying for it."

"Very well," he said. "Ask your question."

"Why are you still single when you own a very successful matchmaking service?"

"I prefer to be," he said.

"That's cheating."

"How do you figure?"

"That's a nonanswer," she said.

"That's the only one I have...so are you still interested?" he asked.

"Maybe. But your answers are going to have to be better," she said.

"I'm holding all the cards," he said.

"Are you?" she asked, knowing he wanted her. She went back over to him and this time she didn't kiss him. Instead she leaned in close, letting her body brush against his. Her breasts were against his chest as she put her hand on his shoulder and leaned close to his ear to whisper directly into it.

"I think I have something you want."

His hands came to her waist and drew her hips forward until his nudged her. She felt his rock-hard erection pressing against her center and shivered.

"We will hammer out the details in the morning," he said. "Be at my office at eight."

She nodded, but he'd already turned on his heel and was walking away. All she could do was watch him leave, but she knew she'd won a victory of a sort. The chemistry between them wasn't something that could be denied and she wasn't going to let him keep pushing her away.

There was no need for her to stay now, so she headed for her car. She knew that it was risky, but she was going to take him up on his bargain—she wanted both the story and the man.

Two

The next morning Nichole dressed to the nines before leaving her apartment on Manhattan's Upper East Side. She caught a glimpse of herself in the mirrored elevator on the way down and the wolf whistle she attracted getting in the cab confirmed she was rocking it.

Normally she would have walked the few short blocks to Conner's office building, but she wasn't taking any chances with messing up her hair or her heels. She'd had one get stuck in a subway grate just last week. If she was bargaining with a master like Conner, she had to bring her A game.

She gave the cabdriver the address and sat back, forcing herself to relax. But her mind was a jumble of last night's kisses and the questions she wanted to ask. She was going to be like Ann Curry—friendly and seemingly open to him but asking the hard questions he didn't want to answer.

She needed to show him that she was here to win. That

she was a serious reporter…but the fact that she'd bargained a question for a kiss might have jeopardized that. She'd just needed entrée, though.

The cab pulled to a stop in front of Conner's building and she paid the driver before getting out. She took a deep breath as she stood and walked toward the revolving door. The street was busy with commuters on their way to the office. She didn't hesitate as she walked boldly into the lobby.

She smiled at the security guard as she told him her name and he got so flustered he dropped his pen. She gave herself a mental high-five and took the guest badge he handed to her. He directed her to the middle bank of elevators.

She got on the elevator and was surprised to find she was on her own on the ride up. When she got to the correct floor, she exited and saw the large logo for Macafee International. When she entered the office, the receptionist took her name and directed her to have a seat in the guest lounge, which she did.

She was offered coffee but she declined. She wasn't here for beverages. She was here for Conner Macafee.

"Ms. Reynolds, please follow me," the receptionist said after a couple minutes.

She was led down a long hallway to an office with Conner's name on the door. It was open and she stepped inside. The first thing she noticed was the size of the office. It was huge, with a wall of windows that overlooked the city. She stood there for a minute with the sun casting a shadow over Conner so she couldn't see his reaction to her.

She walked into the room and found he'd stepped around his desk to offer her his hand.

"Morning, Ms. Reynolds."

"I think we've moved beyond formalities at this point, Conner. Please call me Nichole."

He shook his head. "Bold as ever."

"Did you really think I would have changed overnight?" she asked. "Maybe you aren't as savvy as I gave you credit for being."

He laughed, and the sound made her want to smile. He was fun. If they'd met under different circumstances... maybe. Maybe, what? she asked herself. They would never have met if her friend Gail Little hadn't decided to go to a matchmaker, which had ultimately led to the TV show.

Gail had decided to give matchmaking a try after she'd struggled to find a guy she wanted to really date. As the owner of a PR firm she was busy and didn't have time. When she'd told Willow and Nichole about the service, Willow had jumped on the idea of filming Gail's experiences for her next TV show.

"I'm sure I'll still surprise you," he said.

She was sure of that, as well. "So have you decided to give in to me and just do the interview? Think how refreshing it will be to get it out of the way."

"Please have a seat," Conner said. "I think you must be getting light-headed if you believe that an interview would be refreshing for me."

She walked to the leather armchair placed in front of his desk and sat down. She leaned back and crossed her legs while he watched her. She shifted on the chair and let the hem of her dress ride a little farther up her thighs to see his reaction.

His pupils dilated and he leaned forward, resting his elbows on his desk. Now she knew that she hadn't imagined the attraction between them last night. It had been so strong and so potent she was almost afraid that she'd been dreaming.

"Have you thought more about being my mistress?" he asked.

"I thought I made it clear that I wouldn't do that...I was hoping you'd have come to your senses," she said.

"There is nothing wrong with any of my senses...I'm a man who goes after what he wants, Nichole, and I always get it."

"You've met your match," she said. "I never lose."

"Never?"

Not unless she counted her rather nasty childhood, but Nichole never did. That was the past and she'd been too young to know how to deal with it.

"Not in recent memory," she said. "I'm sure we can come up with something—"

"I already have. I want you. You want me. We both have something the other desires. Now it simply comes down to figuring out how far each of us is willing to go to get it."

She knew he was serious. She could see it in his eyes. "I'm willing to keep the kiss-to-question ratio."

He shook his head. "I'm not. I can't believe you'd be satisfied with that scenario. I'm not the kind of man who multitasks that way. When I have you in my arms I guarantee that you won't be thinking of questions."

A warm shiver slid down her spine. She wanted to be in his arms and she knew it would take very little for him to do what he'd said. She could just give up on the interview and have an affair with him. It would be like lightning hitting dry ground, striking hot, causing a fire to burn out of control until it was put out.

Then he'd go his way and she'd be left alone. She leaned back in the chair, uncrossing and recrossing her legs because she knew it would distract him and give her time to think. But the extra time didn't make her path any clearer. She wanted more than an affair.

She could find white-hot sex if she wanted it, but this interview was once in a lifetime. And she doubted that

Conner would want her if she just gave in. She was going to make him chase her.

"I don't think so, Conner," she said. "You seem like a very competent man and I am more than confident that if you put your mind to it you could answer my questions easily…unless you're afraid of what you might reveal if your guard is down."

She saw that her comment hit its mark as he leaned back in his chair and crossed his arms over his chest. Where before he'd been leaning forward to engage her, now it was as if a barrier had come down between them. Here was the Conner Macafee she'd expected to find.

He didn't like that she'd already found a chink in his armor. He knew the only way to handle Nichole was to show her the door and get on with his life. But he wasn't used to losing and didn't intend to start now. She wanted him and she wanted her interview and he thought it was about time she learned that Conner Macafee didn't back down.

He was going to have her and she was going to acquiesce to his demands. No other solution would satisfy him.

"I have no weaknesses, Nichole, but you are welcome to keep looking for them."

She shrugged delicately and uncrossed her legs again. His eyes immediately tracked the movement. He liked the bit of thigh he kept glimpsing with each shift she made in the chair. He sensed that she was doing it to distract him and probably to turn him on, but he didn't mind.

He liked that feeling of being on the edge of control. It made him work harder to keep his focus and not let her win this round.

Or any round. He didn't like losing and he hated that she was using her innate femininity as a weapon. He knew she was aware of it—well, at least suspected she knew how much she affected him. Duh, right? He'd offered to make her his mistress. She knew he wanted her.

"Everyone has weaknesses, Conner, and I've already figured out one of yours," she said.

"And that would be?"

"You like to be in charge, and if someone threatens that control you don't like it," she said.

He shrugged. "That's not an unusual reaction."

"No, it's not. But you know that I have something you want and I'm not going to give it up easily," she said.

"I'm very glad. I don't like things that are easily attained."

She smiled at him then and he knew that she was savoring the sparring as much as he was. In another world he would have enjoyed knowing her as a woman, not just as a sex partner.

"Good. So here's my thought. We start with my questions—"

"Not happening, honey. No matter how many times you cross and uncross your legs, you aren't going to get me hot enough to agree to that."

"What would get you hot enough?" she asked.

He shook his head, unwilling to reveal that her flirting with him would be enough. "Become my mistress and you'll find out."

"I'm trying to avoid that," she said.

"Why? We both know it's what you want," he said.

She nodded. "It is. But I have my professional integrity to think about."

"Integrity. I didn't know that crashing a party had any high moral value."

"I came as a plus one," she said.

"Whose?"

"Um…"

"That's what I thought. I admire that you're willing to go to any lengths to get this interview," he said.

"How can you be sure of that?" she asked.

"You are sitting here," he pointed out. "As I was saying, I admire your guts. But I think you need to acknowledge that all of your cards are on the table and I'm holding an ace up my sleeve."

"Are we playing for high stakes?"

"Yes, I believe we are. I don't want you to think that my offering to make you my mistress means I don't respect you."

"Sure you do."

"I definitely respect you and I want you. It's the easiest way for us both to get what we want. It's a business arrangement."

"I'm not interested in that," she said. "Perhaps if you knew what I was writing about, it would make you see there's nothing to fear and we could try to have a normal relationship after I write the article."

He wasn't interested in that. He knew from his own feelings on the matter of relationships that he would never marry or settle down. And though he'd never formally had a mistress, in general the women he involved himself with knew he wasn't in it for the long haul.

"I doubt that would work," he said.

"Why? Because I'm not from your echelon?"

He shook his head. "Not at all. It's just that I'm not relationship-minded. Never have been. I saw the dark side of it from my parents' marriage, of course, but also from friends. It's just not to my taste."

"I'd love to quote you on that."

"Well, you can't."

"Honestly, Conner. That is the type of article I want to write. I think even you can see that it's not invasive at all."

"I've already offered to let you interview me if you become my mistress."

"What if I just ask you about the business?"

"You can do that through my marketing department."

"But your marketing department isn't you. I want to know why someone who's so disdainful of relationships would try to set people up."

"In a word?"

"If that's all you will give me," she said.

He bit the inside of his cheek to keep from smiling. He liked that she never just gave in. "Money."

"Money?"

"That's right. There's a lot of money to be made from people looking for that special someone."

"That's so cynical."

He gave a wry shrug of his shoulders. "Obviously I don't run around telling our clients that, but that's my feeling. If the company didn't make money I would have cut it from my portfolio a long time ago."

She leaned forward. "I thought it was a family business."

"That's all you're getting out of me until you agree to the terms."

"What terms?"

"I will answer your questions and you will be my mistress."

"For how long?" she asked.

"A month," he said. "Long enough for us both to still enjoy each other."

"You're not listening to me," she said quietly. "I'm not going to just bow to your wishes."

He stood up and walked around the desk, stopping right

in front of her and leaning back against it, his long legs stretched out so that his well-shod feet were on either side of her. "I won't hold it against you when you do."

She wanted to scream. He was frustrating and so arrogant she wanted to take him down a peg or two. She was tempted to agree to his deal and then back out of it when she got what she wanted. Could she string him along for enough time to get a story?

Could she live with herself if she did that?

She had been brought up in a family where lies—not outright lies but lies of omission—were routine. That was one of the main reasons she'd become a reporter—to expose the truth. So, no, she couldn't lie to him or herself in hopes that she'd get a story without having to pay the price.

"I can't do it," she said. "I have to look myself in the mirror each morning."

He crossed his arms over his broad chest, the sides of his jacket parting so she could see his dress shirt underneath it. This would be so much easier if she wasn't tempted by him. If she didn't want him.

But she knew that anything worth having was worth sacrificing for and she was just going to have to push on and stick to her guns. She'd meant what she said: She had to look at herself every morning and she couldn't do that if she sold her body in exchange for an interview—even if it was a once-in-a-lifetime chance.

"Have you ever paid for an interview?" he asked her.

She sensed where he was going with this. "It's not the same thing."

"Answer the question," he said in that forceful way of his.

"I'll bet you were never spanked as a child," she said.

"What makes you say that?" he asked.

"You are way too arrogant," she replied. "Yes, I've paid a source for an interview."

"Then how would this be different?"

"I get your point—I really do—but we're talking about sex, and there has always been a stigma to paying for it or doing it in exchange for something."

He nodded and leaned forward, putting his hands on either side of her chair so that she was now surrounded by him. His face was just inches from hers and she could see those thick dark lashes of his and the compelling blue of his gaze.

His masculine scent—clean, crisp and spicy—surrounded her. "If I asked you to hire painters to do the walls of this office in exchange for the interview, would you?"

She bit her lower lip. A part of her wanted him to talk her into this. That way she wouldn't have to accept all the blame for the fallout—and she wasn't about to fool herself that there wouldn't be a fallout.

"Of course I would. But I wouldn't just give in. Tell me something. Give me some information that is going to make it worth my while. Sweeten the pot for me," she said.

"I want you."

Those bald words sent a shiver down her spine and made her lean a little bit closer to him. She wanted him, too, but that wasn't the issue. The issue was ethics and pride. She wanted him to want her enough not to make it a business deal.

She licked her lips and noticed that he tracked the movement with his eyes. His nostrils flared as he leaned in even closer and brushed his lips over hers. Just that touch of his mouth on hers sent a pulse of desire through her entire body.

She turned her head to the side. "I want you, too, but I'm not going to give in to physical desire."

"That sounds like a challenge," he said.

"You can try to make it one," she said. "I need to talk about the interview. How about I agree to be your mistress after the interview is done?"

"How could I trust your word?"

She frowned at him. "I'm not known for lying."

"Yet, the day we met you'd snuck into a party to which you weren't invited," he said, stepping back to lean against his desk again.

"True, but that wasn't lying. No one asked to see my invitation."

"Semantics. I want to know I can trust you and the only way I can be assured of that is if we are both giving up something we normally wouldn't."

"God, I'd hate to sit across the bargaining table from you," she said.

He flashed a wicked smile. "I do win a lot, but mainly because I just don't back down."

"I stand my ground as well. How about a little friendly necking in exchange for an interview about the business and the reality TV show? I'll forward you the article before it's published and you can read it to see that I'm keeping my word."

"I'm not interested in making out with you. I want the entire woman when I take you in my arms again. Nothing else is going to satisfy me."

"Okay, we're making progress here," she said, crossing her legs again. "I have something you want very badly and I'm willing to negotiate with you for it. But you have to give a little ground here. What's the bare minimum you are willing to take in exchange for an interview?"

"You bare naked on my desk for fifteen minutes and I'm allowed to do whatever I want to you," he said.

She blushed. She should have been prepared for his

brazen words, but she hadn't been. "Um…no. That's not happening. I don't have the kind of body that would stand up to that much scrutiny."

"You look very fine to me," he said.

She shook her head. Looking good with clothing on was way different than looking good naked, something she realized again and again when she got out of the shower and caught a glimpse of her out-of-shape body.

"Maybe you won't be happy with what you see if I got naked," she said.

"If I'm not satisfied, you still get your interview," he said. "But I know that I'm going to enjoy every inch of you."

She nibbled her bottom lip.

"Come on, red, you know you want to do it. Just give in and say yes, and everything you dreamed of can be yours."

She wasn't too sure she believed that, but a part of her wanted to. She wanted to put her faith in this man who didn't believe in anything, but that seemed like the surest way to broken dreams and a broken heart as well. Because she knew she couldn't separate her heart and soul from her body.

Three

Nichole wasn't a woman who ever veered from a path once she stepped on it. She'd decided to be a journalist and pursued it wholeheartedly. Not just in the workplace, but in her personal life. She'd made choices that kept her single and free to be the workaholic she was today.

She loved her life and didn't regret any of her decisions. But now…she was tempted to make a big change. The kind of change she knew could potentially harm her and her career. She had to be very certain if she agreed to this arrangement with Conner that no one ever knew the details. And she had to be sure she could get her story and keep herself from falling for him.

A tall order. Not impossible exactly, but not easy, either. She just needed time to think and that was out of the question while she was with Conner.

"I can see that your method of negotiating is one of squeezing water from a stone, but I am not going to be pushed into accepting your position as the only one. I know that we can come to terms that will be suitable to both of us."

He walked back around his desk and took his seat again. "I've put all my cards on the table. I'm not going to budge."

"I don't see why not. I'm the one with everything to lose," she said, nibbling her lower lip. She was losing him and she didn't want to.

"Come on, you must see that talking about my personal life in any way isn't easy for me," he said.

She stared at him, feeling a pang of sympathy, remembering coverage of him as a teenager, and she started to soften toward him. But then she glanced up and met his gaze with her own and realized that he was playing her.

"That's not going to work. You're only going to let me see the side of you that you're comfortable with. We both know that you play your cards close to your chest."

"I do. And that's not going to change. Yet, you're an anomaly. I haven't wanted a woman as much as you in a long time, but that could be a danger in itself. I've made my offer and I'm not backing down. If you walk away, I'll probably always have a wistful what-if feeling toward you, but that's life."

She walked over to his desk, perching on the edge of it right next to where he was seated. Though he'd been glib and tried to play her, she knew that he was vulnerable as far as his father was concerned. He didn't want to answer any questions about the past, but she was already seeing how it had defined him.

"If I agree to keep the personal questions to a minimum and just use my own observations…"

"No."

"Conner, you have to give a little."

"I already have," he said, reaching over to put his hand on her thigh.

He rubbed one long finger over the inside of her thigh, tracing a pattern that made sensations flow up her leg to the very core of her. She wanted this man. And all the justification she was trying desperately to find wasn't going to make a bit of difference. She simply wanted to stay. And that was the bottom line.

She could tell herself that she was after the story of a lifetime, but she knew her motivation was rooted in something much more primal.

"I am not going to write something that is scandal-ridden or sensationalized. I think that a lot of people are struggling with finding a mate in today's society, and I'd really like your take on that."

His hand skimmed down her thigh to her knee. She'd had no idea that it could be that sensitive. His touch was warm and brought her an intense awareness each time he moved his hand over her. She stood up and stepped away from him.

"I don't know that you are going to answer any of my questions."

"What do you want me to say?"

"Tell me something, give me a preview of what kind of story I'll be getting so I know I'm not just giving in to your will at my own peril."

He arched one eyebrow at her. "Your peril? That sounds very Victorian and just a tad melodramatic."

"Dang, I was going for more than a tad," she said with a grin. "But seriously…"

"Seriously," he said. "I decided to keep the matchmaking company for two reasons. The first is because it makes me a lot of money. And that's really the only reason that counts. You can't be a businessman in this economy and not give serious consideration to something that is keeping you solvent."

"I agree," she said. This was the kind of information she wanted. He was talking about matchmaking as if it were a widget being made in a factory, and to him it was. "What was your second reason?"

He leaned back in his leather chair and steepled his fingers over his chest. "I want to use it as a vetting tool for my friends. One of my cousins was the target of a gold digger and I hated what she did to him. I didn't want to see anyone else in that situation. Given my own past with my father and the secrets that people keep in relationships, I think having a firm like Matchmakers, Inc. involved in setting up dates is the safest way for people to meet."

She had gotten more from him than she had expected. "That is so cynical. A lot of people meet without doing a background check or having their likes and dislikes tallied and are actually happy with each other."

"I'm willing to bet that they aren't in my socioeconomic bracket. And I'm not saying that to be snooty. There is a different set of variables when you are talking about old money and family fortunes."

"Tell me more about that," she said.

"I'm afraid that's where your sneak peek ends," he said. "If you want any more material for your story, then you're going to have to agree to be my mistress."

She swallowed hard. He had given her just enough to make her want to ask more questions. Her instincts had been right in pursuing him. Conner had the potential to be a career-changing interview.

"What does being your mistress involve?" she asked.

Conner had barely given her any insights that he hadn't shared with friends over the years and was relieved to see that it was enough for her. He understood what she wanted from him and he knew that there were lines he'd always been afraid to cross. Lines that he didn't want to chance letting her know existed because Nichole had proven this morning in his office that she was more than equal to him.

She was willing to sacrifice to get the story and he knew that being in his bed wasn't exactly a hardship. But he also knew that because he'd pushed her into this position he was asking her to do something that was hard for her.

"Being my mistress will involve a lot of pleasure," he said.

She flushed. "I'm not asking for a rundown on what kind of sexual pleasures you will be pursuing with me. I mean, from a logistical standpoint, I have no idea what makes a woman a mistress."

He had no idea, either. He'd never had a mistress before, though his friend, Alexander Montrose, did all the time. Alexander believed that money was at the root of all relationships and the only way to manage relationships was to make them business deals.

"You will move into my penthouse apartment here in the city and be available to me whenever I want you."

"I have my own place and a job."

"For the duration of our arrangement I'd want you to live with me. As you know, I'm the busy CEO of a huge multinational conglomerate, so even though I said you'd be available whenever I want you, we're not talking every hour of the day. Though I think I would want to have you to myself for the first twenty-four hours so I can sate the hunger that has been riding me since I first laid eyes on you."

His words were nothing less than the truth. He had to give Alexander props for the mistress thing. It was so much easier than dating. No coy games or subtleties—just full-on lust. He liked it. He didn't expect to be keeping mistresses full-time in the future, but the more he thought about the idea, the more he liked it.

"I want you, too. What else?"

"I will pay your bills. I might need you to accompany me to a few social events, but given that you are writing an article about me perhaps we should keep that to a minimum?"

"Why? Reporters follow their subjects all the time," she said. "But if I agree to this, I don't want anyone to ever know about our arrangement. I think moving into your place would be a bad idea. There will be doormen and maids who will know I've stayed there."

"What's the alternative?"

"You can come to my house," she said.

"You have neighbors, right? The risk of discovery is just as great. Perhaps you should just disclose that we are dating and let the cards fall where they may after that."

"I'd have to ask my boss," she said. "Actually, that sounds like the best option. Most people won't guess that we have any other arrangement."

"Exactly. A win-win. You get your story, I get your body and we both leave happy."

She tipped her head to the side, staring at him askance. "Happy?"

"I think so," he said. And he'd be in control of the article. He didn't know why he hadn't thought of this before.

"Okay, so I want two different stories from you. The first is strictly about the dating industry and your involvement with the venture. I'll include the stuff you mentioned earlier about vetting gold diggers, that sort of thing."

"Fine. That's no problem at all," he said, glancing at his calendar to see what would have to be moved so he could spend the rest of the day with Nichole. In her arms. It looked like the mistress deal was in the bag.

"The second story will be about the effect your father's betrayal has had on your own dating habits and maybe your sister's. I think it's interesting that she is the home guru yet single."

"No."

"No? To what part?" she asked.

"All of it. I'm not talking about my father. I'm certainly not talking about Jane."

"I want two stories," she said.

"I will not talk about my private life," he said. "There's no merit to it other than gossip and you said you weren't that type of reporter."

"I'm not. I think it's a human-interest story. There are readers out there who want to know what happened to you. They watched you grow up—"

"Too bad. I'm afraid that's a deal breaker for me," he said.

She retreated around the desk, back to the guest chair. He could tell her mind was going one hundred miles an hour trying to come up with something else to tempt him. But he knew the mistress deal was over. He wasn't going to talk about his father—ever.

He never had and never wanted to. His father was nothing more than part of a past that Conner had already forgotten. "I think we're through here."

"Are we?" she asked. "I'm willing to settle for a different type of story."

"The one on dating?" he asked.

"Definitely, but also one on you. Maybe as a corporate raider," she said. "You have done some amazing things with failing companies."

"Yes, I have. But that type of article is more suited to the business pages than the lifestyle section that you write for," he said.

She sighed.

"What's your decision, Nichole? Will you be satisfied with the one article from me in exchange for being my mistress?" he asked.

At this point it was all down to her. He'd live up to his end of the bargain, but he knew there were lines that he'd never allow her to cross. And seeing the way she interviewed him he knew that he'd have to be careful not to reveal too much. He also knew that he was playing a dangerous game by bringing her into his home because reporters were never really off the record.

She wouldn't be satisfied with just one interview with him and one article. But she knew there was more than one way to get what she wanted. And for now it seemed that she should retreat and give this some thought.

It was easy to say that it didn't matter to her if she slept with Conner in exchange for the information she needed. She was a sophisticated, new-millennium woman, but the truth of the matter was she was a bit old-fashioned. And though she often told her friends that she liked to keep her personal life light, so it didn't interfere with her professional life, she knew that deep inside she was afraid to let anyone too close to her.

Living with Conner, even for only a month, would jeopardize that. She was afraid that once she saw what she'd been missing all these years, she might want more.

"I have to think this over," she said. "It's not a decision I can make easily."

"I can respect that," he said. "To be honest, I didn't expect you to agree to it."

"Then why did you make the offer?" she asked.

He shrugged. "There's something about you that brings out impulsive instincts."

"I feel the same way about you," she said. He was different than other men. It wasn't just the wealth and the upbringing that he'd had. It wasn't just that she thought she'd known him from the background research she'd done. It was that she'd been surprised by how different he was than she'd expected.

He gave her a half smile that she was coming to realize was his only way of smiling. He didn't give much away when it came to emotions. He'd admitted to wanting her, but that was lust and she suspected he'd put it down to chemistry. But his real feelings he kept buttoned up.

She glanced at her watch, surprised that she'd taken up thirty minutes of his time. It felt like she'd just arrived. That should be another warning to her. She wasn't herself around him.

"I should be going. I'll get back to you in a few days to let you know my decision."

He stood up and came around his desk, holding his hand out to her. She took it in hers, realizing that although they'd kissed they'd never shook hands. Unsurprisingly, his handshake was firm, conveying confidence.

But it also made her want more. She wanted him to touch her as he had earlier on her leg. She couldn't believe she was going to walk out the door when she wanted him as badly as she did.

"Are you sure I can't change your mind?" he asked as he rubbed his thumb over the back of her knuckles.

"No, I'm not at all sure. But this seems like the kind of thing I really need to think about," she said.

"Thinking is going to overcomplicate it. No one has to know what's between us. How is it any different than a relationship?"

"The agreement. We'd both know that we aren't just dating," she said.

"It's more of a commitment than most relationships."

"Most of yours?" she asked.

"Yes."

"How many dates do you usually have?" she asked. Thinking that she wanted to know personally, but also testing her theory that his father had damaged some relationship skills in Conner.

"Two. You?" he asked.

"Um…about the same. I tend to seek out men who aren't looking for anything long term."

"Why?" He still held her, his thumb making those maddening circles on the back of her hand.

"My career. I don't want anything to derail it."

"Interesting that you are going to walk away from me and the interview that could rocket your career to the next level," he said.

"It is interesting," she said. "But I'm not sure that we'd be okay even if my boss knew we were dating. I can't take a chance of losing everything that I've worked so hard for."

She pulled her hand away. "I…would you reconsider the one-kiss-to-one-question ratio?"

"Not for the long term," he said.

She arched her eyebrow at him. "What does that mean?"

"I don't want you to walk out that door without having one last kiss with you," he said. "I know that once you get back to your office and have time to mull my offer over— you'll more than likely decide I'm not worth the risk."

She suspected by the way he'd worded it that he'd heard that at some time in his past. Was it only his father's secret family that had soured Conner on relationships or was there more to it?

"I doubt I'd ever think you weren't worth the risk," she said impulsively.

"You already do. Or you wouldn't be leaving," he said.

"Touché," she said. She wanted so much more than what he'd offered her. She saw in him a man she could invest herself in. He was a mass of contradictions and she knew that she shouldn't take a chance on him. Shouldn't let him into her heart and mind, but she was afraid it was too late.

"So one last kiss," she said at last.

"Yes," he said, pulling her off balance and into his arms.

Her handbag fell to her feet as she put her hands on his shoulders and looked up into that bluer-than-blue gaze of his. She let herself get lost in his eyes. Forgot that she'd come here for business, but was going to leave with only pleasure.

It was worth it. This little forbidden delight that was Conner Macafee and his kisses.

She leaned up toward him as his mouth slowly descended to hers. He was taking his time, she realized. He didn't want this to end, either. And that made her like him a little more than she already did.

She tipped her head to the side as his mouth moved over hers. His hands caressed her back before settling on her waist and drawing her ever closer to him. He wrapped his arms around her shoulders and drew her closer so they were chest-to-chest. Her nipples hardened as his tongue traced the seam between her lips.

Just that little touch made everything in her body clench as she moistened in her core. Her hands clutched his shoulders as he deepened the kiss. It was demanding and passionate and most of all it said goodbye.

Four

Conner felt more than a little regret as he held Nichole in his arms for what would probably be the last time, but he knew that he had to say goodbye to her. Though she stirred him as no one else had in a long time, she wasn't the right woman for him. And despite owning a match-making business, he wasn't even looking for someone.

Her lips under his were soft and her mouth tasted like the most exotic flavor he'd ever sampled. He was addicted to it, he thought, as he plunged his tongue deeper and deeper. He wanted to sate the hunger for her in this one kiss, but that didn't seem possible.

He craved more. Why didn't he just take what he wanted? It was clear that she wanted him, too, and though she was trying to use that desire as leverage to do a deal with him, in his arms she didn't seem to remember that she was a reporter.

He swept his hands down her back, lingering at the

small span of her waist. He lifted her off her feet and held her against him, feeling her almost melt into him as all plans of deals went out of his mind. All he wanted was for this kiss to never end.

She clung to his shoulders and her breasts rested so softly against his chest. He took two steps backward so he could lean against his desk and continue to hold on to her. Her legs parted and she brushed against his erection as she wrapped those long legs of hers around his hips. He moaned deep in his throat and heard an answering mewling sound from her.

He slid his hands from her knees up to her thighs as he'd been longing to do since she'd walked into his office and perched so femininely in his guest chair. She moved against him, her legs moving around his hips to find purchase with her knees. But the position was awkward and he cupped her butt in both his hands and turned them so she was sitting on the edge of his desk and he was standing between her spread thighs.

The movement pulled their mouths apart and she braced her hands on the desk behind her, looking up at him with those wide, fathomless eyes of hers. Her lips were wet and glistening from his kisses and there was a pretty pink flush of desire on her neck and upper chest.

"One more kiss and then I'll ask my question," she said.

He nodded, not even listening to her words beyond… *one more kiss*. He wanted their next kiss to end with him buried hilt-deep in her sexy body.

He lowered his head again and she started to lean up toward him, but he liked her spread out before him like a sexual offering and stopped her with a hand on her chest. "Stay like that."

"Like this?" she asked, leaning back on her elbows again.

"Yes," he said, his voice sounding guttural to his own ears.

He leaned down over her, taking his time, his hands slowly moving up from her waist to her breasts. He skimmed the edges of them at her side and then moved farther up, tracing the line of her collarbone and the skin underneath. "I love your freckles."

She scrunched her nose up at him. "I don't. They aren't sexy."

"On you they are," he said, lowering his head to lap at one of them. "Are they all over your body?"

He felt her skin heat under his hand and he glanced up, surprised that she was blushing. "Yes."

He growled as an image of her completely naked on his desk, covered only in those freckles, danced in his mind. He reached for the zipper at the side of her dress, but she stopped him with her hands on his and he realized he was in his office.

He stood up and started to walk away from her to cool down, but she pushed her fingers through his and drew his hand to her mouth where she kissed his palm. Then she lifted herself up into a sitting position.

She shifted forward, wrapping her arms around his shoulders, and the motion moved her feminine core against his hardening shaft. She lifted her free hand to his neck and urged his head down toward hers.

The next moment their lips met and once again he found that the only thing that mattered was Nichole and this moment. This time she didn't just let him devour her mouth, she was aggressive and passionate in the kiss as well—more of a participant this time. He felt her move his hand to her breast and then her hand fell away and he was cupping her through her bra and dress.

He had a realization that Nichole was bold and brash in her reporter mode, but the woman was a bit shier and softer. He liked that. He wanted to have that woman in his arms. But he knew that he could never separate the two.

This was goodbye and he needed to remember that. He wanted this complex woman, but these stolen moments in his office were all he was ever going to have.

He rubbed his forefinger over her breast as he plunged his tongue deep into her mouth and when he felt her nipple bud against his finger he concentrated his touch there. She shifted in his arms and then he felt the strong suck of her mouth on his tongue.

His hard-on strained against the front of his trousers and he used his other hand at her waist to draw her closer to him. He rubbed himself against her and felt her rock her hips against him.

He tipped his head to the side to take more of her mouth, wanting to see this through to climax. Nothing could stop them now. Their bodies knew what they wanted and now that they were touching their minds had stopped arguing for anything else.

He pulled the fabric away from her body and slipped one finger under to feel the softness of her skin.

There was a loud rap on the door and Conner stepped away from Nichole. He realized that he couldn't let his body take over. This was probably how his father had gotten into the mess he'd made of their lives.

"Just a minute," he called, turning back to see that Nichole was struggling to get up off the desk. There was a strong blush on her face and she looked unkempt. He gestured to his washroom. "Why don't you take a minute to repair the damage I did."

She nodded and walked across the room. As he watched her go, he knew that he'd had as much of Nichole as she could afford to give.

* * *

Nichole was losing control. She realized how little she had over herself and Conner. He was making a mockery of her and the entire interview. She had to stop compromising herself this way. She closed the door of the executive bathroom behind her and locked it.

She saw herself in the mirror. Her hair and clothes were disheveled and she hardly recognized the woman staring back at her. She met her own gaze and gave herself a frown.

"You worked hard for your career and you are about to let a man derail you," she said to herself sternly, reaching into her purse for her makeup bag.

"Dammit, Nic, you can do this. You can beat him." She reapplied her lipstick and put some powder on her nose. Then she straightened her clothing, turning to make sure she looked as good from the back as she did from the front.

On the plus side, she could definitely count on the fact that she had kept Conner off balance. But her plan to beat a strategic retreat had almost backfired. She'd underestimated her own desire for him. And that ticked her off. She'd always been in control in her attractions with other men.

She'd learned early on to keep a level head, but Conner somehow had gotten through her guard. She knew that she'd never be able to sleep with him and still be the calm, cool reporter she prided herself on being.

And without that who was she?

She leaned in close to the mirror, searching for the answer, but the woman looking back had no answers. She realized that she was taking too long in here. She didn't want Conner to think that she was scared to come back out or to even let him guess he might have gotten the upper hand in their negotiations.

Which, even she had to admit, he had.

She opened the door and found that he was standing across the room staring out the plate-glass windows at the city below. She walked over to stand next to him. Having grown up in Texas with lots of wide-open spaces, she always found it a little breathtaking to see the cityscape spread out before her.

"I think you owe me one answer," she said.

"I believe I do," he said. His voice was firm and calm, but he seemed subdued around her now.

She wondered if their embrace had shaken him as well. It was easy to look at him and see a man who was always in control of his life and his environment, but she had seen little chinks in that facade.

"Fire away," he said.

But she was still muddled and the questions she wanted answers to had nothing to do with an article. She wanted to know why a normal relationship was out of the question with him. Why he'd only consent to take her as a mistress when it was clear he wanted her. But that wasn't the question to ask now.

She cleared her throat. "Let me grab my notebook."

"By all means," he said, walking back to his desk and sitting down.

It was hard to believe he'd been kissing her so passionately only a few minutes ago. Sitting before her was a totally different man...the man she'd been expecting him to be from the beginning.

Given that this might be her last chance to question him, she wanted to make it count. She took a deep breath and asked the question she really wanted an answer to. One that was highly personal and one that, depending on the answer, could give her the backbone for her entire article.

"I've read finance magazines that say your business acumen is very much like your father's. Are you still single today because that's not the only area in which you and he are the same? Do you fear making the same mistakes he did?"

His mouth tightened and she knew that her probing questions were making his hackles rise, but he owed her. She'd given him much more than the one kiss he'd asked for. And she was fairly confident that he was an honorable man.

"I'm not going to answer that other than to say that many people have said my business instincts and my father's are the same, and aside from the fact that we both have helmed Macafee, I can't see any other similarities."

"My question isn't really about the business, Conner. I want to know if you're afraid of being too much like him."

His mouth tightened and for the first time she felt a shiver of something almost like fear running down her spine. He wasn't a man she wanted to be at odds with.

"No comment."

"No comment?"

"Did I stutter?" he asked flippantly.

She stood up and walked to his desk. Placing both hands on the surface of it, she leaned over toward him. "We had a deal. I more than held up my end of the bargain."

He steepled his fingers together and stared at her over the top of them.

"You did, red. I never expected for things to...get so hot, so fast."

"Me neither."

He gave her a little half smile as he dropped his hands to the armrest on his chair.

"I'm not asking for much. I won't print a direct quote from you on this in my article, but I do want to know because I think that is part of the cornerstone of who you are today."

He shook his head. "I'm afraid I can't answer that."

"*Won't* is more like it. You owe me," she said.

"Ask a different question," he said. "I'll allow you time to come up with one."

"I have asked my question and I expect an answer. You didn't bargain for any approval over the question I wanted to ask. I'm a reporter. I need the answer."

"Reporters are only privy to certain parts of their subjects' lives. As I'm sure you know."

"Yes," she said. "But certainly a mistress has more rights."

"No," he said. "I'm afraid she doesn't. You only have the access that I grant you."

She was stunned speechless. And so angry she wanted to punch him. He had tricked her. She doubted that if she went to bed with him he'd hold up his end of the bargain he'd wasted her morning trying to get her to agree to.

"Excuse me?" she said. For the first time he heard the tang of her Texas accent coming through.

"I'm not giving you carte blanche," he said.

"I didn't set any limits on that embrace," she said.

"But you did," he pointed out, remembering his strong desire to see the expanse of her creamy, freckle-covered skin.

"We're in your office," she said. "We can't go too far."

"Yes, we are," he conceded. "But I believe you were attempting to do what I'm doing now. We are each limiting the access the other has to what they want. Trying to give away just enough to keep this going."

She nibbled on her lower lip. "I can see where you're coming from, but what you just said makes it almost impossible for me to trust you. I want this to work. I think that readers have an interest in *you* and not just your company."

"I don't care about the personal aspect. How would you feel if I asked you personal questions?"

"Go ahead," she said. "I'm an open book."

"Why are you still single?"

"I told you—I'm a workaholic. I love my work."

"Me too," he said. "There's your answer."

"Ha! That was my answer. We both know there is more to you than that."

"And I know there is more to you than what you said. Something must have hurt you in the past to make work your sanctuary."

He saw by the way she narrowed her eyes that he'd hit the nail on the head with that observation. "So? I'm not in the public eye."

"Neither am I," he said.

"That's not true. You're in the newspapers all the time and your sister has a cooking show...I think if we walked out on the street right now you'd be instantly recognizable. No one would know who I am. And that's the reason why this article is so relevant."

"I don't believe there is any interest in me beyond gossip," he said. "I've given you the answers I am going to."

"You can be a hard-nose, can't you?" she asked.

"And you can be a pit bull when you aren't getting your way," he said. "We are too similar. We both expect to win and in this situation it's simply not going to happen."

"I guess you think you're the winner?" she asked.

"I intend to be," he said.

"Well, then, there isn't anything more to say, is there?" she said, standing up and gathering her bag.

He knew immediately that he'd made a huge mistake in how he'd worded that last bit. But she'd struck a nerve with her question. It was exactly as he'd feared when she'd asked to interview him. The information she wanted was too personal and he wasn't about to let anyone—even someone as rocking-hot as Nichole—have that kind of access to him.

"You didn't win," she said, opening the office door and looking back over her shoulder at him. "I'm not giving up."

"I wouldn't expect anything less," he said.

She walked out, hips swaying, making him wish his secretary hadn't knocked on the door when she had. But there was no going back and changing the past; he knew that better than most. God knew there were a lot of things he'd change.

He sat back in his office chair and wondered if their encounter would affect her coverage of the show and of Matchmakers, Inc. He hoped she was professional enough not to let it.

He knew she was. She wanted the interview with him and she was going to keep working on different angles to get it. There was a part of him that was looking forward to her next move.

There was a knock on his door. "Come in."

"Your next appointment is here," Stella said. Stella was in her mid-forties, a single mother of two college-aged boys. She'd been his secretary for the last ten years and he relied on her a lot to make sure the office ran smoothly. "Shall I send him in?"

Conner glanced at the calendar on his computer screen. He wanted to groan. It was Deke, one of his old boarding school buddies whose family fortunes had been tied to a Ponzi scheme. Now he was in need of a job.

"Yes, please do," he said. "Stella, don't let this meeting run more than thirty minutes."

"Yes, sir. I never do," she said with a smile. Which was why she'd knocked on the door earlier.

Conner didn't know what to do about his old friend. A part of him understood Deke way more than he wanted to. He knew what it was like to see your family name in the papers with scandal attached to it.

He stood up as Deke entered. He was six foot and had dark curly hair. He'd rowed crew at boarding school and still had the upper-body strength of an athlete. But Deke's family money had meant that he'd spent the last fifteen years jet-setting around the world. He had no real-world skills.

"Hello, Deke," Conner said, holding out his hand.

Deke shook it. "Hey, man. Thanks for seeing me today."

"No problem. I meant to call you, but I've been busy. What can I do for you?" Conner asked.

Deke looked uneasy for a moment, then gave him a smile. "I have an investment opportunity for you."

Conner suspected as much, which was why he'd put his friend off as long as he had. He walked back to his desk, gesturing for Deke to take a seat in the chair that Nichole had recently occupied, and then invited his friend to explain the opportunity to him.

While Deke talked, Conner's mind wandered back to the time of his life when he'd been in Deke's shoes. Luckily, Conner had been young enough to readjust, but Deke was an adult, used to a certain standard of living.

"I don't have many skills, but I'm damn good at sailing and my wife suggested we start up one of those barefoot-type vacation cruises. All my assets have been seized, so I don't have my old yacht, which is where you'd come in. If you agree, I'd like you to invest in one yacht that I can use for these high-end sailing vacations."

Actually, it was a great idea. Conner asked a few more questions and Deke produced a business plan with some solid numbers in it. Seemed Deke had married a woman from a working-class background who wasn't afraid to help her husband out of a bad situation.

Conner agreed to invest in the company from his private funds and not Macafee International's. Deke was a happy man and once he left Conner felt strangely alone.

He knew it was his own choice to be where he was, but hearing Deke talk about his wife and her ideas had made him long for something he never had before.

Conner wondered if Nichole would react the same way if her man got in trouble. He didn't know. But then he didn't know anything about her except that he wanted her.

Five

Nichole dropped by the set of *Sexy & Single,* the reality matchmaking television show featuring Conner's company. She had been writing a blog about the daily goings-on of the show behind the scenes. Lots of information and maybe just a little gossip.

The producer of the show was one of her closest friends, Willow Stead. Willow came over the moment she walked on the set, which today was a private balcony near Central Park West. The other part of their trio, Gail Little, had been the first bachelorette on the television show. And Nichole had been happy to report that Gail had tamed her match, the Kiwi billionaire Russell Holloway, and they were engaged.

The second couple featured on the show, fashion designer Fiona McCaw and billionaire game developer Alex Cannon, were also engaged. Willow said her show was on a roll.

But Gail was back to her job in PR and the weekly drinks were the only excuse the three women had to get together anymore. Which was to be expected. A part of Nichole wished that she and her friends had more time for each other, but life was busy.

"Hey, lady!" Willow said, coming over to hug her.

"Hey, you," Nichole said, trying for her usual cheeriness but it was hard since she'd only just come from Conner's office and he'd...well, he'd left her shaken.

"Rikki Lowell is a handful. I can't imagine how she runs a successful party planning business. She's so demanding," Willow said about the show's latest bachelorette. She linked her arm through Nichole's. "I'm so glad I'm not the matchmaker."

Nichole smiled. "She has a reputation for demanding perfection."

"I've seen it. I don't think Paul is going to measure up in her eyes."

"He's a partner at one of the top corporate law firms in the country. He should meet at least some of her standards," Nichole said. She'd interviewed him and found him to be charming, smart and very sweet. "Is he too nice for her?"

Willow threw her head back and laughed. Nichole noticed that Jack Crown, the celebrity host of the show, glanced over at them. He'd gone to the same high school as the three friends, which made them all meeting here a bit of a small-world type thing. But he'd been two years ahead of them and Nichole hadn't remembered him at all. "Don't look now, but Jack Crown is watching you."

"Is he?" Willow asked without turning around.

"Yes, he is. Why is he watching you?"

"I have no idea," Willow said.

"Liar."

Willow blushed. "We can chat later."

"We will. I'm going to call Gail and tell her to bring a bottle of wine and we are coming to your place tonight."

"Fine, but anything I say must be kept off the record," Willow said.

"It always is," Nichole reminded her friend. Her comments made Nichole wonder if that was part of why Conner thought he couldn't trust her. Was he afraid that she'd reveal all sorts of intimate personal details about him in her article?

"Do you ever worry that I might slip something you said to me into an article?" Nichole asked Willow.

Willow wrinkled her forehead. "No. I know you wouldn't do that. I was just teasing."

Nichole nodded. "I guess we've been friends for so long we trust each other."

"We do indeed. I don't trust him though," Willow said.

"At least he's cute."

"Ha. Like cute counts for anything."

"Can you believe we went to high school with him? I certainly don't remember him roaming the halls. But then I was pretty much in the library all the time and something tells me Jack didn't even know the school had one."

Willow laughed, but there was something quiet about her as she turned to stare at Jack. "I did know he was at our high school."

"I'm going to ask you more about that later," Nichole warned as Jack started to walk over to them.

"I've got to run," Willow said and left before Jack joined them.

Nichole smiled up at the show's celebrity host. "What's new?"

"I got to fly with the Blue Angels last weekend," he said with that big toothy grin of his, which she noticed didn't quite reach his eyes. And his eyes…well, they followed Willow as she walked away.

"For one of your shows?"

Jack was the host of nearly half a dozen shows that aired on three different networks.

"Yes. *Extreme Careers,*" he said. "Want an exclusive interview with me?"

"Ha, you talk to every reporter. There's nothing exclusive with you."

"What can I say?" he asked, again with that grin. "I liked the article you wrote about Gail and Russell. I was worried the backstage stuff might be sensationalized…"

Nichole shook her head. "Gail is one of my closest friends. I'd never print anything to hurt her."

"I didn't realize that. So you're from Frisco, Texas, too?"

"Yes. I don't remember you at all, so if that's what you're thinking, we're in the same boat," she said.

"I wondered about that. Why didn't we ever run into each other? A pretty redhead like you…I definitely should have noticed you in high school," he said.

"Probably because I spent most of my time in the library or in Mr. Fletcher's classroom. And I don't think you did either of those things."

"Did you write anything I might remember?"

"Only if you found the weekly lunch menu fascinating," she said.

He laughed. "Oh, that was you. I'd like to talk to you later for *Extreme Careers.*"

"Okay, but being a society reporter isn't considered 'extreme' at all."

"I know. I was hoping you could use your contacts to help me find a war reporter."

She nodded. "I know a couple of guys who've been to

the Middle East. I'll ask around and see if they'll talk to you about it."

"I don't just want to talk to them, Nic. I'd like to go over there with a reporter and do some frontline shooting, too," he said.

She didn't think that any of the reporters she knew would want to be on a reality television show, but she'd been wrong about Gail wanting to be on one. "I don't know if anyone will agree to that."

"Let me talk to them. I can be very convincing and, if not, there's more than one way to get the story I want."

Jack left and she talked to the bachelor and the bachelorette for a few minutes before leaving herself. One of the things Jack had said continued to resonate with her. There was more than one way to get a story and if Conner wouldn't talk to her, she might have to look into the other members of his family, especially Jane Macafee. She was in the spotlight and might have some insights into Conner that Nichole could use for her story.

Conner sent three calls from his sister to voice mail and narrowly missed her when she showed up at his office for a surprise visit. Finally, when she tweeted about him, he couldn't ignore her anymore. He picked up his office phone and dialed Janey's number.

"It's Conner," he said when she answered.

"I know it is. Why are you avoiding me?" she asked. "I wanted to find out what happened with that redhead reporter."

"Nothing," he said. Jane was as bad as could be when it came to snooping into his personal life. Besides, Nichole was the last person he wanted to discuss with anyone in his family.

"Nothing? You spent a lot of time with her for nothing."

"She was…difficult," he said.

Jane chuckled. "Good. Sometimes I think life is a little too easy for you."

He wished. "Did you just call to harass me?"

"You called me," she pointed out. "I tweeted about you."

"Which I have repeatedly asked you not to do," he said. Whenever she mentioned him on the internet or on her show he got slammed with emails through the company website, asking if he was on Twitter or Facebook.

"Sorry, bro, but if you ignore me you must face the consequences."

"So what did you want?" he asked.

"I'm having a dinner party tomorrow night and have an odd number of guests so I need you to come. It's at eight so you'll be done with work."

"Are you filming it?" he asked. One time she'd been doing her cooking show and he'd shown up unaware that the dinner was going to be taped. He had left without saying a word to her, but they'd had a huge fight over it later. Janey didn't understand why he still had such an aversion to the press. In her mind what had happened with their dad was over years ago. But it was different for Conner.

"No. I think we both remember what happened the last time I did that."

"Thanks, Jane. I'd love to come to dinner then. Eight?"

"Yes," she said. "Did you talk to the reporter?"

"Only to get her to leave. She wanted to do a story on Dad and that old scandal," he said, which wasn't quite true, but he didn't want Jane talking to Nichole. His sister could be stubborn once she had an idea about something.

"Oh, that's too bad. I thought she was doing a piece on the television show that Matchmakers, Inc. was part of."

"She is. But she also wanted to delve into the personal

side of it. Stuff like why do I own a matchmaking firm if I'm determined to stay single."

"A question Mom and I have pondered many a time," Jane said.

"Um…you're single, too. Would you like to delve into your reasoning on that?"

"I haven't met Mr. Right," she said.

"I don't think you're even looking," Conner said. "I do want you to be happy."

"I am happy. And I suspect you are, too. We aren't like other people who need a spouse to be fulfilled," she said. "We learned a long time ago to depend on ourselves—and each other, of course."

"Of course," he agreed. He hadn't realized that Janey felt the same way he did. He'd tried his best to shield her from the worst of the fallout with their father. "I thought I protected you from most of the family drama that made me such a loner."

"You did. You have always been the best big brother a girl could ask for."

"The best…that's not what you tweeted a few minutes ago."

She laughed as he'd hoped she would. It bothered him that his sister was as closed-off to interpersonal relationships as he was. He'd adjusted to living alone and not letting anyone get too close, but Janey was gregarious and always had a group of friends around her.

"Love you," she said.

"Love you, too, brat. Is Mom coming to this soirée of yours?"

"No, she has a board meeting for her charity. She said if you didn't agree to come she'd call and put the screws to you."

"You two always team up, don't you?"

"If we didn't, you'd stay shut away in your office like some sort of hermit and then, when we finally did see you, who knows what you'd look like."

"Now you're just being silly," he said. He liked that Jane had retained most of her upbeat personality. She'd always been a giggling little girl, but after their father left and the scandal broke there were times when Conner thought he'd never hear his sister's laughter again. Luckily, over the years they'd moved on and slowly that specter of pain from their father had dulled.

"Yes, I am. See you tomorrow night," she said and hung up the phone.

Conner spent the rest of the afternoon in meetings and pretending that he didn't notice that Nichole Reynolds had tweeted about him right after Jane had. He knew that social media was the wave of the future, but personally didn't care for it.

Which was why he continued checking to see if Nichole tweeted anything else. He didn't know why he was so obsessed with that woman. Sure, she could kiss his socks off and just the thought of her in his arms gave him a raging hard-on, but otherwise she was just like every other woman and reporter he'd ever met.

He was kidding himself. He knew that she was different and he wanted to see her again. Except that he'd done everything in his power to make sure she didn't come back.

He knew that he'd said some callous things to her the last time they were together. A better man would call and apologize or send flowers or jewelry, but he couldn't be that man...*wouldn't* be that man. As Janey had said, life was easier when he only depended on himself, and he wasn't about to risk that for Nichole Reynolds, no matter what her effect on him.

* * *

Willow lived in Brooklyn in one of those brownstones that were going for millions of dollars back before the beginning of the recession. She had waited and watched the property she wanted until the market had gone soft and she'd been able to buy it. That was one thing about her friend that Nichole envied. Willow had patience. She would wait as long as it took to make something happen.

Nichole knocked on Willow's door just as another cab pulled up and Gail Little stepped out. Gail smiled and once again Nichole was struck by how happy her friend looked. The two women hugged and said hello. Willow opened the door with her cell phone to her ear. She gestured for them to come in.

"So why did you call this emergency meeting?" Gail asked as they both entered Willow's foyer and walked down the short hall into the kitchen.

"Willow is keeping a secret about Jack Crown," Nichole said, opening the cabinet to get out three wineglasses. Gail opened the bottle of chilled Chardonnay she'd brought and poured three glasses.

"She is?"

"I'm not," Willow said, entering the room. "I knew him in high school."

"How come you never mentioned it before now?" Nichole asked.

Willow sighed and took a long swallow of her wine. "Let's sit down if you're going to grill me. I ordered a pizza and it should be arriving in fifteen minutes."

"Good," Gail said with a big smile. "Plenty of time for you to tell us all about your Jack."

"He's not my Jack…I tutored him when he was a junior."

"What year were we in?" Nichole asked.

"Freshman."

"That must have been humiliating for him," Gail said.

Willow flushed and looked down at her glass. "I have no idea. He needed help in English. That was all."

It didn't take reporting skills for Nichole to know there was a lot more to the story than Willow was letting on.

"Yeah, right," Gail said.

"Why didn't you ever mention him to us?" Nichole asked.

"Because he was just another kid I was tutoring. You guys didn't want to hear about that."

"Was he cute back then?" Nichole asked. "He had to be. He has what scientists call the golden triangle. His face is perfectly symmetrical. He is beautiful," Nichole said.

"Don't let him hear you say that. His head might explode," Willow said.

"That sounds like a lot more than just his old tutor talking. What happened between the two of you?" Gail asked.

Willow finished her glass of wine and poured another. "He…he was just a teenage boy and I was a stupid teenage girl who thought that just because he was nice to me in private we were friends in public."

"Oh, Will, I'm so sorry," Nichole said, putting down her glass to go and hug her friend. Gail joined them, rubbing Willow's back.

"That's too bad. He seems like a fun guy now," Nichole said.

"You'd probably like him," Willow said. "He keeps things light, the way you do."

Nichole wasn't too sure she kept things light anymore. She certainly hadn't been able to do that with Conner. She wanted something more with him, but wasn't sure she trusted herself.

"He's not my type," Nichole said, mentally comparing

Jack to the clean-cut handsomeness of Conner. He'd suddenly become her fantasy man. No surprise there, given the chemistry that sizzled between them.

"Since when?" Willow asked.

"You don't understand what I liked in my boy toys," Nichole said.

"*Liked?* Do you want something else now?" Gail asked. "This is exciting. Do you have a man in your life? One you're serious about? I think you were grilling Willow to keep us from asking you about your life."

Nichole bit her lower lip. "Truthfully, there is a guy, but it's complicated and I really don't think anything is going to come of it. But I sort of wish something would."

"How could it be complicated?" Willow asked. Then she gasped. "Oh my God, is he married?"

"God, no. Do I seem like the kind of woman who'd date a married man?"

"You said it was complicated, and you don't let anyone get too close," Gail said gently.

"I meant—never mind, I don't want to talk about it," she said, feeling hurt that her friends thought she'd get involved with someone who was married.

"I'm sorry," Willow said. "I guess you cut a little too close with your questions about Jack and I wanted to strike back. I know you'd never have an affair with a married man."

Nichole nodded but she wasn't ready to forgive yet.

"Don't be mad, Nic. We can't always choose the people we're attracted to. We never thought you'd do anything with a married man, but that doesn't mean you wouldn't fall for one," Willow said.

"You're right about not being able to choose who we fall in love with," Gail added. "I never thought I'd fall in love with a playboy. I mean Russell just wasn't my kind of guy…but then somehow I started caring for him."

"He *was* your kind of guy. You just couldn't see it because of all the flashbulbs that surrounded him," Nichole said, letting go of her hurt.

"I had a crush on Jack in high school," Willow blurted out. "It ended badly and I've been wanting to get back at him ever since."

"Get back how?" Nichole said.

"Some kind of humiliating revenge. I thought I'd gotten past it, but I haven't."

"Oh, dear," Gail said.

"Oh, dear? What are you, ninety-two?" Nichole asked. "Our BFF is contemplating revenge. We need to use stronger words here."

Gail shook her head. "Willow isn't going to change her mind no matter what we say, and I have a feeling it's going to be—"

"Complicated!" Willow said. "Just like Nichole's situation."

The women laughed as the doorbell rang. Once the pizza was on the table, talk turned to the TV show and Nichole let Conner and how he complicated her life dominate her thoughts. There had to be another way to get her story and still get him. Because she wasn't ready to let him slip away just yet.

Six

Conner worked up until the last moment when he could leave and get to his sister's apartment but still be fashionably late. If Nichole had been here to see him, she'd have realized that he wasn't a social animal. He dreaded parties and other social gatherings because he didn't do small talk.

Yeah, right. He didn't like them because he hated being around strangers who might know too much about his past. He didn't know how Jane was able to survive her life in the spotlight. There were always people who wanted to prod her about the past and ask questions about how it had felt to go through that public humiliation.

Something that Conner hoped never to relive. When he was a block from Jane's apartment, he remembered that he hadn't picked up flowers and didn't have a bottle of wine. And there was no way he could show up at the home of America's leading hostess without a hostess gift. Janey would nail him for it.

"Stop at the corner, Randall," he said to his driver. "I need to get a bottle of wine."

"Yes, sir," Randall said.

Conner ran into the corner store and bought the best bottle of wine they had available. It wasn't a pricey vintage, but he knew it was one his sister liked. As he was waiting in line to pay, he caught a glimpse of Nichole's face next to her byline in *America Today* that the woman in front of him was reading.

Glancing over the woman's shoulder he saw that the article was about Jack Crown's latest daredevil stunt. Conner had met Jack since he had been brought in to host the reality TV show, but he hadn't had a chance to get to know the other man.

"Why don't you buy your own copy?" the lady said, folding the paper in half and putting it on the counter.

"My apologies," he said, embarrassed to be taken to task by the woman. But he wasn't going to read the society column of any paper. It was little better than gossiping and he wouldn't do it. Though, if he'd been pressed about it, he would have had to admit that Nichole's writing style was very inviting. He'd wanted to read more.

But not today. He paid for his wine and shoved the sexy, redheaded reporter out of his mind as he got back in his car. Randall drove the rest of the way to Janey's high-rise but when he pulled up to the curb, Conner was reluctant to get out.

"I'll text you when I'm ready to leave," he said. "It might not be too long."

Randall laughed. "I'll be in the garage waiting for your text."

Conner took the elevator to the penthouse, entering the code that would take him straight to his sister's place. When he exited the elevator, he had the uneasy feeling that he hadn't timed his entrance to be as late as he'd hoped. The first person he saw when he walked into her hallway was Palmer Cassini.

"So, she roped you into this as well," Palmer said.

"Sadly, yes. But I was corraled because of an uneven number of guests."

"She used a different technique to get me to come tonight. How have things been?"

"Good. Business is business, but we're turning a profit and in this economy that's all anyone can ask for."

"You say it like you're blasé about it, but I know that you're in the black because of your savvy and leadership," Palmer said.

Conner tucked his hands into his pockets and tried to look nonchalant, but Palmer had hit the nail on the head. Conner wasn't about to let years of hard work go down the drain because of a downturn in the economy.

"Where's my sister?"

"In the kitchen with another guest. One I suspect she may have invited for you," Palmer said.

"Should I leave now?" Conner asked jokingly.

"I wouldn't. She's a very sexy woman."

"Do you wish she'd invited this mystery woman for you?" Conner asked. He'd be more than happy to bow out of the dinner and let Palmer go after her.

"Not at all. I shouldn't tell you this, but I'm very interested in your sister," Palmer said.

"You are?"

"Yes, but she's stubborn and refuses to let me get too close."

"Don't mess around with Jane," he said. "If you hurt my sister…"

"You'll come after me, I know. But it is she who hurts me. She doesn't want anything serious to develop between us and every time I get too close she shuts me out…the way she did at the Fourth of July party."

He sympathized with his friend. It was hard to court a difficult woman. And though he wasn't courting Nichole, she was difficult and he did want her. He clapped a hand on Palmer's shoulder. "If it's meant to be, it will happen."

"I'm not sure I want fate on my side. She can be a cruel mistress," Palmer said with a laugh. "Come on, let's go join the women."

Conner wasn't too sure he wanted to, but hopefully whoever Jane invited would take his mind off Nichole, even if it was only for tonight. He needed to put the attraction to her in perspective. He'd been working too hard. That was probably why he'd been so consumed with her lately. She was, after all, the only woman he'd kissed and held in his arms recently.

Of course, he was going to be thinking about her all the time. In fact, he was doing it again, he thought. The woman in the kitchen even sounded like Nichole as he walked toward it. But as soon as he crossed the threshold and entered the kitchen he realized it wasn't his mind playing tricks on him.

Nichole was standing next to his sister, helping her assemble some kind of hors d'oeuvre and laughing at something Jane had said.

Remembering the last time he'd seen her, only a day ago, and how she'd left his office, he couldn't help believing that she was here for revenge. She had gone after his sister when she hadn't been able to get the dirt on him.

Of course a woman like Nichole would never understand that Jane wouldn't give him up. His sister was very loyal and knew better than to talk about their past with any reporter, no matter how charming she was.

"Uh-oh, my brother doesn't look happy to see you," Jane said.

"I told you he wouldn't be," Nichole said.

He handed the bottle of wine to Jane and gave her a kiss on the cheek. "Nichole, I'd like a word with you in private. Jane, I'm using your study."

He turned on his heel and walked out of the kitchen. He heard the sound of Nichole's carefully measured footsteps behind him as he entered Jane's study and waited for her to follow him in.

He gestured for her to enter the room and carefully closed the door behind them. Then turned to her. "What the hell do you think you're doing here?"

Nichole had suspected that Conner wouldn't be pleased to see her here, but she'd never guessed that he'd be so angry. "Having dinner."

"Don't be flip. It was cute the first time we met but now, not so much," he said.

"I'm not being flip. I'm here to have dinner," she said. "I had no idea that you'd be here."

"I'll bet you didn't."

"What exactly do you think I'm plotting to do?" she asked. "Your sister is friends with one of my BFFs...actually you know her, too. Willow."

"So you asked Willow to get you close to my sister?" he asked.

"Not at all. I want an interview with you, Conner, not with your sister. She's funny. She thinks that we'd make a great couple but that you're letting the fact that I'm a reporter keep you from seeing my charms—her words," Nichole said.

"I can see your charms," he muttered under his breath,

rubbing the back of his neck. "So you're not here to dig up dirt on me?"

"Nope," she said. "And I'm insulted that you'd think I'd do something like that. I'm a reporter with ethics. I don't make up stories or dig through trash cans to find leads. When I write my story on you, it will be because you gave me an interview," she said. To be honest, she was insulted, and who wouldn't be. But more than that, she was hurt. She had the feeling that Conner was doing everything he could to keep from being attracted to her, and if that meant that he had to make her into the bad guy, then she guessed that's what he'd do.

"I'm not going to stay for dinner. Your sister is delightful, but you are not the man I thought you were," she said, turning to walk away.

He grabbed her elbow and tugged her off balance until she fell back into his arms. "I'm sorry."

"What?"

"I'm sorry," he said. "I felt cornered by Janey and then seeing you just added fuel to the fire. I was happy to see you, I *am* happy to see you. Dammit, Nichole you are a complication."

"I said the same thing about you earlier. I don't know why you can't simply agree to the interview and then we can get it out of the way."

"I can't do that. I've sworn I'd never give an interview."

"But you can bargain with me?" she asked.

"It's the only card I have," he admitted. "It's the only thing I can say to keep you interested in staying here with me."

"You could try asking me to stay."

He shook his head. "I can't. Then you'd know how much I really want you."

She wrapped her arms around him and hugged him

close, putting her head on his shoulder. "You make things so hard."

"I do, don't I?"

She pushed away from him, taking a step back. "Why is it so hard for you?"

"Just between us?" he asked.

She nodded, realizing that he was more vulnerable than she ever would have guessed.

"You're not like the women I've dated," he said.

She arched one eyebrow at him. "That sounds like a line."

"It isn't. You are so fiery and passionate about your work. You don't let anything stand in your way, but when I hold you in my arms I can tell that you are equally passionate with me. I want that, but…"

"But what?"

"You can also seem all-consuming," he admitted.

She understood what he was trying not to say. She suspected that he was afraid, just as she was, of letting him get too close. They were both, in their own ways, used to being alone, and meeting someone of the opposite sex with this much chemistry was a threat.

There was a knock on the door before it opened. Jane stood there with two cocktail glasses in her hands. "I'm sorry I didn't tell each of you that the other was coming."

"It's okay," Nichole said.

"We'll talk later," Conner said.

But Jane just handed a cocktail glass to Nichole and then hugged her brother. "It's your own fault for refusing to say what happened between the two of you. I knew there was something going on."

She saw Conner's face tighten and though Nichole knew Jane had been trying to help, she'd just done the one thing guaranteed to drive Conner further away from her. He prided himself on being aloof, but he couldn't be if everyone saw them as a couple.

Dinner wasn't as awkward as he'd feared it might be. First of all, the only people at the party were the four of them and since Palmer and Jane were two of his favorite people, Conner found it easy to relax. But that just kept him on guard a little more. He didn't want to inadvertently give anything away to Nichole that she'd use later.

Once the meal was served, Jane was in her element at the head of the table. As the hostess, she kept the cocktails flowing and the conversation moving.

"So, Nichole, inquiring minds want to know. Why did you decide to become a reporter?" Jane asked after Palmer finished telling them a hilarious story about his first polo game when nerves had gotten the better of him and he'd fallen off the horse.

"I always wanted to be one. I think I saw myself as a Nancy Drew type when I was little," she said.

"Oh, I liked Nancy Drew, too," Jane said. "But solving crimes isn't the same as being a reporter."

Nichole put her fork and knife down and took a sip of her drink before she leaned forward. "When I was in high school, I had Mr. Fletcher for freshman English and he was the sponsor of the school newspaper. He liked my writing and told me I should join the newspaper staff. I did. I liked it," she said.

"What did you like about it?" Conner asked, fascinated at learning more about her. Suddenly she wasn't just a nosey reporter—hell, she'd never really been just that— but now she seemed more real to him.

"My family had a lot of secrets growing up. Stuff we didn't talk about with each other or with anyone outside the family. That's not healthy. I liked the fact that my job was to find out the truth, to report and let everyone know what was going on. It was such a change from my home life that I was addicted to it, I think."

"Sort of like me and making this perfect lifestyle on television," Jane said. "In real life I'm so not perfect."

"I'd have to disagree," Palmer said.

"You don't know me well enough to disagree," Jane said, wrinkling her nose at Palmer.

"I'm trying to," he said with a laugh.

Nichole picked up her fork and toyed with the asparagus on her plate. Conner wanted to know more. What kind of secrets had she learned to keep? He doubted it was anything like the ones his father had kept. But when she looked up and caught him staring at her, he smiled gently in her direction and she blushed.

"What made you decide to do a cooking and lifestyle show?" Nichole asked.

"I always liked to make my room a retreat. So I started learning how to sew and craft things. And then when we had to leave our home in the Hamptons there was a six-month period where we didn't have a cook—do you remember?" she asked, turning to her brother.

"I do," he said. "You started cooking for Mom and me."

"Well, Mom is an excellent fund-raiser and bridge player, but the woman cannot cook," Jane said with a laugh.

"Sounds like you found your calling," Nichole said.

"I did," Jane admitted. "I just liked the feeling I had when Mom and Conner ate my food. I made them happy and life was good while we were sitting around the table."

Conner wished Janey wouldn't talk like that in front of Nichole. He had no idea what she'd print about him or his sister. He had nothing but her word that she'd only use what she learned in an interview.

"I feel the same way about being at my mother's kitchen table," Palmer said. "We have a cook but my mama likes to cook for me and my brothers. There is such a feeling of love in the dishes she prepares."

"What about you, Nichole?" Jane asked. "Are you like me or your mom?"

Nichole nibbled her bottom lip, something he realized she did when she wasn't sure what to say. "I don't know. It's just me at home and I don't cook much for myself. But I think maybe someday, if I have a family, I'd like to create something special like you or Palmer's mom do."

He didn't like the thought of Nichole having a family someday and he didn't want to acknowledge why it disturbed him. He knew he wouldn't be the man in her life and he didn't like the thought of another man being with her.

"That's sweet," Jane said.

"What about you, brother?"

"What about me? I'm never getting married. I like my freedom too much."

"I don't believe that's true, but that's a conversation for another night," Jane said.

"What about me, darling Jane? Don't you want to know what I'd want?"

"No. I know what you want and it sounds like someone else's dream," she said. "How about some dessert?"

Jane pushed her chair back and stood up. Palmer watched her go and Conner had to admit that he felt sorry for his friend.

"I'll help Jane with the dishes," Nichole said, gathering the remaining plates before she went into the kitchen.

"Why is your sister such a stubborn woman?" Palmer asked, his Brazilian accent heavier than normal. "I could make her happy."

Ordinarily Conner wouldn't have offered any advice. He

made it a policy to stay out of Jane's personal life so that she'd stay out of his. But he liked Palmer and he wanted his friend to be happy. "She doesn't trust happy."

"What do you mean?"

"The last time she was truly happy and trusted someone, it blew up in her face."

"You mean your father?" Palmer asked.

"Yes."

"There's been no man since then?" he asked.

"Not that I know of," Conner said.

"Then I will have to work twice as hard to show her that she can trust me," Palmer said. "That I am nothing like your father was."

"That's going to be hard," Conner said. "Our father did a lot of damage."

The door to the dining room opened and Nichole was standing there. He knew she'd heard his comments and he hated that. If she were just a dinner party guest, he could pretend it meant nothing, but she was a reporter bent on digging up his past.

Jane came back with a coffee tray and a fake smile. She was overly animated and it was almost painful to watch her pretend to be the perfect hostess now when they'd seen her genuinely enjoying herself earlier. The tension between Palmer and Jane was palpable.

Nichole must have felt the same way because as soon as dessert was eaten, she glanced at her watch and said she had an early morning and had to go.

"I'll walk you out," Conner said. He hated that years later his father still had the power to hurt both him and his sister. It wasn't fair that neither of them had found a way to heal from those lies.

"Okay," Nichole said. "But I don't think it's necessary."

"Maybe he wants to be in your company," Palmer

said. "Sometimes a man just wants to prove himself to a woman."

"Or maybe I'm ready to leave as well," Conner said.

He got that Palmer was talking to Jane, but he didn't want Nichole to get any ideas about what he had in mind for them.

Seven

Nichole was tired and just wanted to get home. What had started out as a fun and interesting night had become a little tense as she rode down in the elevator with Conner. Especially when he reached out, pushed the stop button and turned to her.

"Everything that Jane said tonight was off the record. I don't want to see that showing up in your column tomorrow morning," he said.

She sighed and wanted to punch him hard in the stomach. "I already said I have ethics. When are you going to get it? I don't write about what my friends say at their dinner parties. Your warning shows me that I was completely wrong about you from the beginning."

"What do you mean?" he asked.

"I thought maybe we could have a chance as a couple."

"I don't want to be a couple. I want to have you as my mistress," he said.

"I know," she said, reaching around him to start the elevator car in motion again. "I really do have an early meeting and since we've had the mistress discussion before, I hope you won't mind if we skip it now."

He leaned back against the wall of the car and stared at her with that bright blue gaze of his. "Don't be offended. I can't take any chances."

"Why not?"

He crossed his arms over his chest. "When I was nineteen and just starting to take over the reins at Macafee International, *Business Week* sent a reporter to interview me. He was about my age and easy to relate to. He spent a week or so following me around at the office and I let my guard down and talked openly with him. He printed things that weren't part of the interview itself and I learned the hard way that there is no such thing as *off the record*."

She was angry with the reporter who had abused Conner's trust and a little sad for the young man he'd been at that time. "I'm not like that."

"You say that, but then you also told me you'd do anything to get this story. And then I show up at my sister's house and there you are…it doesn't look good," he said.

"She invited me," Nichole said carefully, enunciating her words, though the anger she'd felt earlier about his attitude had disappeared. She had caught a glimpse of the private side of Conner and she wasn't about to let that slip away. He was a man with a lot of complicated emotions. Tonight had proven that. And though he was arrogant and demanding, she was beginning to suspect that was all a ruse he used to keep from being hurt again.

"Why are you looking at me like that?" he asked.

"Because I'm just getting the feeling that I've barely scraped the tip of the iceberg that is Conner Macafee."

"Iceberg? I thought I'd proven I was anything but cool as far as you were concerned."

"Oh, you're red hot when I'm in your arms, but you seem so forceful and solid underneath that it'd be easy to accept you as just a man who wanted a mistress. But then the water moves and I see something hidden in the depths of you..."

"That's pretty deep. I'm really not all that. I'm just a guy who likes to get his way and right now my way would be you in my bed."

"If only that were all you were asking," she said.

"Would you have a one-night stand with me?" he asked.

That point-blank delivery struck her the same way his initial demand that she be his mistress had—with a thrill she couldn't deny, at least to herself, and then a bit of sadness because she genuinely liked him and wanted so much more than just one night.

"Would you sit down to an interview with me?" she asked.

He shook his head. "You haven't changed my mind."

"Are you sure?"

The elevator doors opened and they stepped out into the lobby of the building. There weren't many people there and Conner took her arm and drew her to a quiet corner.

"Actually, I'm not sure. Tonight when you were talking about secrets...I want to ask you about your childhood. Would you be willing to open up to me about it?"

"Maybe," she said. She didn't like talking about her own secrets. It made her mad at herself that she still couldn't break the habits that were ingrained in her since childhood.

"What if I gave you a kiss?" he asked.

She had to smile at him. "You can be a scamp, you know that?"

"Yes," he said. "If sheer willpower won't convince you to give me what I want, I'm not afraid to use charm."

"Is this still a game?" she asked, because she needed to know before she let herself fall any deeper for him.

He pulled her closer to him, wrapping one arm around her waist and leaning in so that his breath brushed her cheek when he exhaled. He smelled the way she remembered him, spicy and delicious, and she wanted to rest her head against his chest and just let him wrap her senses in comfort.

"I'm not sure," he admitted.

With another guy that wouldn't be enough of an answer, but with Conner it was more than she expected. He was so guarded. So used to protecting himself and keeping everyone at arm's length that she felt even that tiny admission was a treasure.

"I'm not, either," she said, looking up at him.

"How are you getting home?" he asked.

"A cab, why?"

"I have my driver waiting. Can we give you a lift?" he asked.

"Why would you offer?" she asked.

"I'm not ready to say good night yet."

"Why not?" she asked.

"You sound so suspicious," he said with a laugh. Pulling out his cell phone, he typed a quick message.

"Well, with you I've learned to be."

"Don't be," he said, cupping his hand under her elbow and leading her to the exit. "I just want a chance at uncovering your secrets."

Conner was happy that Nichole had accepted the offer of a ride from him because he wasn't ready for the evening to end. Randall said nothing as Conner gave him Nichole's address; the driver just piloted the car through the evening Manhattan traffic.

Nichole sat back against the leather seats of the Rolls Royce Phantom. Conner stretched his arm out along the back of the seat and toyed with a strand of her hair, wrapping the silky lock around his finger and then letting it unravel.

"You're making my life difficult," she said at last, turning toward him.

"I know," he said. If he'd let go of his convictions and say yes to having an affair with her, life would be easier, but he didn't know for how long. He suspected it would only last until he got her into his bed and then he'd be back to the same distrust he had now.

"What kind of secrets did your family hide?" he asked. He wasn't going to play around and pretend that he didn't want to know about her past. Knowing the person she was might make it easier for him to trust her. But it would also make it easier for him to figure out what kind of pressure to apply to make her cave in to his desires.

"You still want to know about that?" she asked.

"Stop stalling. You know I want to know every detail about you. And I tried researching you on the internet the other day and couldn't find anything but your column and the articles you'd written."

"You researched me?"

"My attorney advised me to," he said, deadpan.

She narrowed her gaze on him and then started laughing. "Dated a few crazies?"

"No, I was joking with you. I wanted to know more about you. Find out what made the woman behind the reporter tick."

She shifted around in the seat, turning so she faced him.

"There isn't much to tell. My family's secret isn't too bad or too dark. It was more damaging the way we dealt with it."

The way she downplayed it told him that wasn't true. "What was it?"

"Depression. Severe depression that makes the person feel like they should kill themselves," she said.

"Which family member?" he asked, not liking the sound of her secret.

"My mom. She has medicine she can take to control it, but it makes her sort of a vegetable so she hates it. My childhood was a roller-coaster ride and we could never discuss Mom's periods of blueness. That's what she called it."

"What about your dad? Surely, he said something to you," Conner said.

"Not really. He was at work most of the time and he was the one we'd hide it from. I'm an only child, so it was just my mom and me at home," Nichole explained. "When I was little my dad traveled a lot for business and that always brought on my mom's depression."

Conner remembered the one thing she'd said earlier that he'd let pass. "Did she ever try to kill herself?"

Nichole pursed her lips and turned to look out the window. He could see the reflection of her drawn face in the car window as they passed under the street lights. "Once. My dad had to be called home. I was fourteen. He didn't travel after that and my Aunt Mable moved in with us to watch her while he was at work."

"Did that help?"

"Yes. She's much better now," Nichole said. "See, it wasn't so bad. It's not like she hit me."

"Well, it's good that you weren't physically abused, but you still saw things that no child should. Who found your mom?"

"When she tried to kill herself?" Nichole asked.

Conner nodded. He suspected that she had, but he wanted to hear the story from her lips.

"I did. I...I thought she was sleeping and tried to wake her. When I couldn't I panicked and called my dad. I told him everything. He took control and called 911. I just sat on the floor next to my mom holding her hand. It was really horrible," Nichole said.

Conner put his hand on her shoulder to comfort her and then drew her into his arms. "I'm sorry."

"It's not your fault, but thanks. Dad and I had a long talk about everything and after that Mom was much better. You know," she said, turning to look up at him, "it was then I realized if he'd known from the beginning how bad Mom was when he was gone, he would have stopped it sooner. That helped me decide to be a reporter. Maybe I can find out some facts that will spare someone else."

Conner wondered about that. It had been a reporter who'd uncovered his father's second family and that had hardly helped him or Jane. The only thing that could help in those situations were adults who behaved like adults. Parents who understood that their first duty was to their child. Something his father hadn't ever understood.

"I'm glad that you found a career that could help you," Conner said and he meant it. Though it was the one thing that was keeping her from being his.

The car slowed to a halt in front of a walk-up apartment building.

"We're here," she said.

Conner grabbed her wrist before she could open her own door to get out. "I've tried to get you out of my mind."

"Me, too," she said.

He smiled. "Would you please consider negotiating with me again? I don't think I'm going to be able to sleep or even have a moment's peace until we get this resolved."

She nibbled her bottom lip and he leaned in to kiss it.

"Stop chewing your lip to bits. You know you want to figure out something between us."

"I do. Want to come up and have a drink? We can discuss it in my living room instead of in the backseat of your car," she said.

"Yes, I would like that," he said.

Randall got out of the Rolls and opened the back passenger door. Nichole slid out of the car. Conner joined her on the sidewalk, telling Randall he could have the rest of the night off.

"Um…how do you plan on getting home?" she asked.

"A cab."

Conner followed Nichole up the three flights of inside stairs to her apartment. When she unlocked the door and opened it, she stood there, hesitating for a minute. He knew that once they moved forward into her place, something would change between them.

This would be the first time they'd been somewhere private together. Not his mother's party or his office or his sister's apartment, but Nichole's home. And there was the promise of intimacy in that.

Nichole figured that of all the men she'd invited back to her place, Conner was the most dangerous. He wasn't one of her just-for-fun guys, that was for sure. She couldn't even blame that on him. She was the one who wanted something more.

She'd like to say it was because of the chemistry between them, but she knew the mere chemistry was for boy toys. What made her want more with Conner was the depth she'd glimpsed in him. She knew there was more to him than met the eye and her subconscious was driving her to uncover this man's mysteries.

She led him into her apartment, which was a respectable size for New York but not nearly as large or glamorous as Jane's had been. She put her keys on the table in the hallway and as soon as he entered she closed the door behind him.

"Welcome to my home," she said. "I've had enough alcohol tonight so all I'm serving is soft drinks or coffee."

"Coffee sounds great," he said.

"The living room is through there," she said, pointing down the very short hallway. "Make yourself comfortable while I get the coffee. Do you take cream or sugar?"

"Both," he said.

She walked away without looking back. She needed to regain her focus, maybe recall that she was trying to find out about him, not tell him every detail of her own life. But she knew that, somehow, if talking to him about her past helped him relax and eventually trust her, then she'd bare it all.

Hell, she'd seriously considered becoming his mistress for the story. Now she thought it might have been easier to sleep with him than to reveal the parts of herself she'd rather keep hidden.

She had one of those Keurig machines and absolutely adored it. She made coffee at all hours of the day and night now, and she could change blends without having to throw out the entire pot of coffee. Willow called the Keurig her dealer. And Nichole had laughingly agreed that coffee was definitely her drug of choice.

She made two cups in the matching I ♥ New York cups she'd bought when she'd first come to the city as a student. She put them on the serving tray that had been her grandmother's, then placed the sugar dish and creamer next to the cups, along with spoons and napkins, and finally made her way to the living room.

She'd heard if you didn't look at a full cup it wouldn't spill, but the path of coffee stains on her carpet from the kitchen to her home office proved otherwise.

She had expected Conner to be sitting down on the couch or in her recliner. Instead, he was standing up studying the pictures that hung on the wall of her living room. He was in front of a photo of her with her parents on graduation day.

Though he didn't say anything, she could almost sense that he was remembering what she'd told him about her mom earlier. "Seeing her like that, it's hard to believe she has any problems."

"Absolutely," Conner said. "She looks happy and proud of you. They both do."

"As I said, I'm an only child so I was always their entire world."

"That's good. I can stop thinking of you as the Little Match Girl."

"Thank God. I never want you to think of me that way. Come and get your coffee," she said.

She set the tray on the coffee table and then sat down in her recliner so she wouldn't be seated right next to him. His arched eyebrow told her he knew what she was up to.

He added milk and sugar to his drink while she wiped up the coffee that had spilled out of her cup and pooled on the tray.

"Do you?" he asked, holding up the coffee mug.

"Huh?"

"Love New York?"

"Oh, yes. I do. I was so terrified when I first got here, but that quickly faded," she said. "What about you?"

"I don't especially love it. More like tolerate it," he said. He took a sip of his coffee and then leaned against the back of the couch, crossing his legs.

As he settled in there in her house, Nichole knew the last thing she wanted was for him to go home tonight. She wanted to be curled up next to him now and then make love to him in her queen-sized bed later. But the only way she could do that was if she figured out how to get her story *and* her man.

She thought about the night and the dinner they'd shared. She hadn't minded talking about her past when she'd known that it was only Jane, Palmer and Conner who would know about it, but if she'd thought that one of them might blog or tweet about what she'd said she would have felt differently.

"I think I get what you meant when you asked me how I'd feel if everyone read about my personal life," she said.

"Do you? Given your past, I think you'd want to keep it hidden," he said.

"That's what I mean. But most of the people who know me can guess that there is something in my past that keeps me from being in a committed relationship."

"And that has any bearing on this how?" he asked.

"Give me a second. I'm fiddling around with the problem between us. If we can find a way for me to write the story without asking you any direct questions about your past, would that be okay?"

He leaned forward, resting his elbows on his knees. "I thought the golden ticket was me talking about the past."

"It is. But I can see now that you'll never do that and I don't know if I even want to write that story anymore. I'm thinking more that I can interview you about the TV show and then just observe your interactions with your family. I won't ask them any questions and anything they say to me will be off the record, but my own personal observations might make interesting reading."

Conner stood up and walked over to her chair, resting

his hip on the arm as he leaned down over her. "Let me get this straight. You'll observe me and my interpersonal relationships with my family but only interview me about the show?"

"Yes," she said, tipping her head back to meet his eyes with her own.

"In exchange for being my mistress?" he asked.

She hesitated. She'd hoped to just have a relationship with him without the mistress arrangement, but it looked as if that was something Connor had to have.

Eight

Conner was reluctant to agree to anything with Nichole, but at this point she'd become such an obsession that he had no choice but to figure out a way to have her. He knew nothing else would satisfy him. He stood up and walked away from her chair.

Her apartment revealed a woman who had deep roots and connections to the people in her life. Every photo was genuine. No staged smiles, no fake emotions. He wanted to trust her, but the desire he felt for her made it harder for him to do it.

Was he giving her a free pass because he wanted her in his bed or was he seeing the signs of a woman he could truly trust? He just didn't know, and he was afraid to make the wrong choice.

He had no problems acknowledging his own fears. He knew that he had weaknesses; if you pretended you didn't, you were only fooling yourself and headed for a big fall.

He turned to look over his shoulder at her. She chewed her lower lip and stared pensively at him. He should just let go of the mistress thing, but he couldn't. He wanted her to be his completely and only as his mistress would he have the freedom to make their every meeting about sex.

In his head it seemed like sex was the way to go. The one thing that would make a relationship with her manageable. Otherwise, he'd be tempted…hell, he already was tempted by everything about her. And he knew that he didn't want to allow her to mean too much to him.

"You haven't answered my question," he said.

She shook her pretty head, the red hair brushing over her shoulders and her bangs falling forward to cover one eye before she tucked the hair back behind her ear again.

"I'll do it," she said, "but only if you agree to let me capture my own observations about your family and that dynamic. I think that will add a personal touch and that's what my readers expect."

He turned back to look at the wall of photos in her apartment. If he agreed to let her observe his family, he'd leave them all vulnerable. That wasn't acceptable. How could he manage it?

He was so close to having Nichole and everything he wanted. And he was a damn smart man at the bargaining table, no matter who sat on the other side of it. He knew there had to be a way to make this work.

"How would you observe my family? With me present?" he asked.

"Yes, when we went to functions they were also attending. I assume you'd bring your…"

"Mistress," he said. "If you can't say it, how can you agree to be it?"

"I'm going to say *girlfriend*. We can both pretend it means mistress."

"Don't do that, Nichole," he said. "Make sure you know that what we are going to have will be temporary. It's stamped with an end date."

She nibbled her lip again.

"You're going to chew your lip raw," he said.

She stopped. "You're right. Why does it matter what I think about our arrangement?"

"Despite what you might think of me," he said, "the last thing I want is to see you hurt."

"That makes two of us," she admitted.

"Good," he said.

"So you'll do it?"

He would be able to control the amount of access that Nichole had to his family. He didn't know for sure if that would be sufficient, but in the end he knew he was going to agree to this. He would manage her and her access to his life. He'd been doing that with the media since he'd turned seventeen, so he wasn't too worried about that.

"Yes," he said.

"Okay…now what?"

He laughed at the way she said it.

"Well, we have to seal our deal."

"In writing?"

"I don't think so. That kind of document could end up in the wrong hands," he said. "How about with a kiss?"

"A kiss…just one kiss?" she asked, standing up and walking over to him. "One kiss is never enough."

"No, it's not. So let's say a kiss, but take whatever we get," he said.

She nibbled her bottom lip again when he opened his arms to her. She just stood there staring at him and he wondered if now that he'd agreed she was going to back out.

"Second thoughts?"

"Yes," she said softly. "And third and fourth thoughts. It

all comes back to you and the story. I want you both. But a part of me is sure I'm going to regret this."

He closed the gap between the two of them and pulled her into his arms. He hugged her gently, trying to reassure her, yet he honestly had no idea how this would turn out. He hoped by making her his mistress he'd be able to control the influence she had over his life and ensure that his emotions didn't get engaged. But this was Nichole and nothing had gone according to plan since she'd shown up uninvited at his family's Fourth of July party.

"I will do my best to make sure you have nothing to regret," he said.

She tipped her head back and stared up at him with that pretty gaze of hers. "That's the worst part. I know your intent isn't to hurt me, just as mine isn't to do any damage to you, but I'm not sure that as much as we are trying to make this a business arrangement that we'll succeed."

She had a point, but he'd made up his mind and she'd agreed to his terms. He wasn't letting her go or giving her a chance to back out.

"We'll both just have to do our best," he said, lowering his head and taking the kiss he'd wanted all evening.

Nichole was glad to stop thinking and just enjoy Conner's embrace. Tonight hadn't gone exactly the way she thought it would but she'd gotten the one thing she'd set her mind on. Why, then, wasn't she happier?

She was in Conner's arms, enjoying his ravishing kiss, but her mind was reluctant to let her relax and just enjoy it.

"I can tell you're still thinking," he said. "I'm insulted that my kiss hasn't distracted you."

"You shouldn't be. I'm just…oh, I don't know. This is crazy. I spent my entire adult life building my career and trying very had to expose the truth, and I've just agreed to do something that feels like a back-alley deal."

"There's nothing back alley about it. It's inevitable that you and I are going to have an affair. I don't know about you, but I don't feel this kind of chemistry with every woman I meet."

She had to admit that was true. "I guess that's part of why I'm so shy about seeing this through. I know you said by making it a business agreement we could mitigate the possibility of both of us getting hurt, but I don't know—"

"You can't worry about the ending right now when we are just at the beginning," he said.

He'd kept his arms around her and his words were dissolving her fears. She tipped her head back and he lowered his mouth to hers once again. This time, as their lips met, she let her fears melt away.

She wrapped her arms around his shoulders, as his hands slid down to her hips, drawing her closer to him. They were pressed chest to chest, hip to hip, and she wished they were even closer.

His tongue thrust into her mouth. She sucked on it and then let her hands find the buttons of his shirt. First she loosened his tie and then she undid the first few buttons so she could slip her hand under the cloth and touch his warm flesh. There was a faint dusting of hair on his chest and it tickled her fingers as she caressed him.

His hands were busy cupping her butt and drawing her closer to his groin. She felt him hardening against her as he thrust his hips into the notch at the top of her legs. She moaned in the back of her throat.

He tore his mouth from hers and she felt his lips against the side of her neck. He dropped nibbling kisses down the column of her neck, lingering to suckle the spot at the base where her pulse raced.

She tugged his shirttails from his pants and wrapped her arms around his bare torso. She wished she was bare-chested as well, wondered what it would feel like to have him pressed against her right now. She lightly scratched a pattern down his back along the line of his spine, touching him with growing passion as his mouth found hers again.

She let him control her. As if there was any other re-action she could have toward him. He was dominant and that came through in his embrace. He sucked her lower lip into his mouth and gently rubbed his tongue over it. She was trembling with passion. Sensations radiated from the kiss to the tips of her breasts and then lower as moisture pooled between her legs.

"I want you," he said, in a husky whisper into her ear.

"Me, too," she said.

He lifted her in his arms and carried her toward the couch. He sat down and set her on his lap. Her legs were to one side, one hand on his stomach, her other hand on his shoulder. He tipped her head up and kissed her again.

His hands swept over her body, pulling her blouse up until he'd exposed her midriff. His hands were warm as he rubbed them over her lightly. She shifted around so that she was reclining on his lap like some kind of sexual offering. Then he shifted their position on the couch until she was lying beneath him and he straddled her hips.

His shirt swung free, both sides falling away from his long, lean chest. She massaged his pectorals before she traced the light line of hair that tapered across his stom-ach to where it disappeared into his pants.

He moaned her name in a way that made it sound like ecstasy. She felt an answering tingle deep inside her own body. She shifted her legs until she could sprawl them open and then grabbed his hips to draw him down toward her. But he held fast.

"Not yet," he said. "There is still so much of you I haven't explored."

She didn't want this first time to last forever. She wanted him to continue overwhelming her senses until she came hard and repeatedly.

"I don't want to wait."

"Too bad," he said. "You're my mistress. What I say goes."

He leaned down and bit lightly at the flesh just above her left breast. She glanced down to see that he'd left a tiny mark.

"I don't want you to forget you're mine," he said.

"There's not a chance of that happening," she said. She reached between them for his belt and started to undo it. But he stopped her by wrapping his hands around her wrists. He drew them up above her head and held them there.

"Not yet," he said, firmly. He pushed her blouse farther up her body until her breasts were revealed encased in a flesh-colored bra. It was more practical than sexy, but the way that Conner looked at her told her he didn't need lace to be turned on by her.

Her nipples were hard and beaded against the material. Conner plucked at her right nipple with his free hand then lowered his head to put his mouth over her left one. She felt everything inside her clench at that touch. Her hips arched up toward his and, as he continued to suck on her nipple through the fabric of her bra, she arched her hips. Desperately trying to reach his.

She tugged on her arms, trying to free her wrists, but Conner held her firmly without hurting her. There was such decadence in the way he held her and touched her. She was shivering on the edge of an orgasm and she wasn't sure what she wanted at this point.

One thing she wanted was to feel his erection pressing against her, but she knew he wasn't going to lower his hips until he was good and ready.

"Conner..."

"Yes..."

"I'm going to come."

"Not until I tell you to," he said.

"I can't wait," she said, her words gasped out as she kept lifting her hips. He lowered his mouth to her breast again and let go of her hands as he thrust his hips against hers. Even through their clothing, the tip of his erection hit her clitoris and she shuddered as her orgasm washed over her.

Conner hadn't meant for the kiss to go as far as it had, but he'd been wanting her for so long it was all he could do not to open his pants and thrust himself deep inside her straight away. Holding her while she came was a double-edged sword that made his desire even stronger.

But he hadn't come to her house prepared to make love to her and he wasn't about to chance accidentally getting her pregnant. He wasn't thinking too clearly when he felt her hands between his legs and her fingers moving over his fly. She'd undone his belt and the next thing he knew her hands were on his hard-on.

She slid her fingers over the tip and his hips jerked forward, a bead of moisture slipping out. She rubbed her finger over it and then brought it to her lips to lick it away.

Her other hand pushed his pants and underwear over his hips and then he felt her cupping him. She squeezed gently as she rose up and found his mouth with hers. She kissed long and slow and deeply.

He leaned down over her, letting his bare chest brush over her bra. He reached underneath her body and undid the catch and then pushed the fabric off her breasts. Her skin was lightly freckled and he leaned down to kiss each of the freckles before slowly making his way to her strawberry-colored nipples.

He tongued them as she continued to caress his erection. He wanted her and could think of nothing but getting inside her silky-smooth body.

He let his hands skim lower to the waistband of her skirt and unzipped the side fastening before pushing it down her legs. She shifted underneath him until the skirt was completely off.

He thrust his hips forward and felt the smoothness of her skin underneath him. She felt so soft and womanly and as he stared down into those chocolate-brown eyes of hers, he felt something else change inside of him. Something more emotional, and that jarred him. Nichole was the one woman he'd met who made him react this way. This strongly. And he didn't know if making love to her was such a smart decision after all.

But his body wouldn't let him back down now. Wise or not, he wanted her. He wasn't going to be able to breathe again until he was buried hilt-deep in her curvy body with those long legs of hers wrapped around his waist.

He also knew he didn't want to rush this first time with her. He stood up, toed off his shoes and stepped out of his pants and underwear.

Before he reached down to lift her in his arms, he asked, "Where's your bedroom?"

"Down the hall," she said, gesturing to the left. He held her high in his arms and walked the short distance to her room. "In here." She reached out and hit the light switch as he entered the room. It was flooded with soft light from two bedside lamps. Her bed was queen-sized with an aqua-blue comforter on it. He set her on her feet and slowly finished undressing her, taking his time to enjoy each new patch of skin revealed.

"Do you have a condom?" she asked.

"Yes."

"Thank God," she said.

Once she was naked, he lifted her onto the bed and laid her back against the pillows. The aqua comforter was the perfect backdrop for her red hair and her creamy freckled skin. She kept her knees bent, but he saw the red hair that covered her most intimate secrets. He shrugged out of his shirt and stood there looking down at her.

He took her ankles in his hands and drew her legs down and apart from each other. She bit her lower lip.

"You can't be nervous now," he said, slowly drawing both hands up her legs, caressing her soft, smooth skin. He lingered on her knees and watched as gooseflesh spread up her legs as he moved his touch slowly higher toward her center.

"I'm not," she said. "I just expected you to be on me quicker."

"I don't like to rush things, even pleasure," he said.

He took a moment to put on the condom, then crawled onto the bed between her spread legs. He put his hands on either side of her chest and leaned down over her. He kissed her softly on the side of her neck and then moved his mouth lower to trace the globes of her breasts, first with his kisses and then with his tongue.

Her hands came up and tunneled through his hair, holding his head to each breast as he tongued one nipple then the other. Supporting his weight on just his right elbow, he used his left hand to draw a line down between her breasts over her ribs to her belly button.

He traced a circle around and around it, watching the red flush to her skin deepen. Her own hands were busy caressing him and he enjoyed every pulse of desire that she drew from him seemingly effortlessly.

He was on the knife's edge and he knew that no matter how much he wanted to prolong the moment until he entered her, he was fighting his own instincts. He wanted her with a red-hot desire that was hard to contain.

It was only the fact that he also wanted to taste every inch of her that allowed him a modicum of control. He lowered his head and traced the circle of her belly button with his tongue.

Her hands were back on his head as her hips rose on the bed.

"I need you," she said, her words raspy and drawn out.

They sent a shiver down his spine. She writhed underneath him as he shifted his position so he lay between her legs, his elbows on either side of her body.

He slid one hand up to caress her shoulder and neck before pushing his fingers into that thick red hair of hers. He kissed her deeply, pushing his tongue into her mouth as he pulled his hips back and then slowly thrust his hips forward.

He slipped slowly into her. Inch by inch, he went as slowly as he could and it felt so good. Finally his willpower gave way to his body's demands and he pushed himself all the way in. He was buried in her silky-hot body and it wasn't enough. He needed more. He started thrusting harder and deeper, urged on by her cries for more.

Her legs came up and wrapped around his hips. Her nails dug into his shoulder blades and she cried out his name as he felt her tightening around him. His own guttural cry of release followed a second later.

He kept thrusting, spilling himself inside her until he was spent. He collapsed against her chest, careful to keep her from bearing his full weight. Sweat covered both their bodies and he felt the minute kisses she dropped on his shoulder. He wrapped his arms around her and, keeping their bodies together, rolled to his side so he could hold her properly.

He kept his eyes closed, knowing he was hiding, but at this moment he didn't want to see her face or talk to her. He needed the silence to pretend that nothing had changed between them when he knew that everything had.

Nine

Nichole slept restlessly. She wanted to blame it on not being used to having someone else in her bed. But what weighed on her mind was the fact that Conner had only agreed to be her lover because of their bargain. She had vivid dreams of her boss finding out how she got Conner's story and firing her.

She finally got out of bed at six, just before her alarm went off. Conner appeared to be sleeping. She slowly went to the bathroom, trying to be extra quiet so as not to wake him. She didn't want to face him this morning. She knew she shouldn't leave without waking him, but she wanted to.

Part of her was very afraid of what he'd say to her. Of what she'd say... Last night had been more intense than she'd expected. But then nothing with Conner had gone exactly according to plan since the moment she'd met him.

She carefully closed the door to her tiny bathroom and reached over to turn the shower on to get the water hot.

She glanced at herself in the mirror and shook her head. She didn't look any different.

Maybe she was overthinking the entire arrangement with Conner. There was nothing tawdry about having slept with him. She'd had one-night stands before and she knew that as long as both she and her partner were on the same page, no one would get hurt. So why then was this bothering her so much?

Steam started to fill the tiny room and she pulled back the shower curtain and got inside. She started to wash when she heard the bathroom door open.

"Morning, Nichole," Conner said, his voice sounding raspy with sleep. She stood there frozen with her loofah in one hand and the shower gel in the other.

She shook her head. He knew she was in there and probably had guessed that she was naked. Why was she being so silly?

"Morning," she said. "Sorry if I woke you. I have an early meeting."

"Not a problem. I would normally leave you in peace in here, but this is the only bathroom and I, too, have an early meeting so I need to wash up."

"That's fine," she said. Oh, man, she'd come in here to hide from him and now he was here. But at least she didn't have to face him. *Not yet.*

"What's your day like?" he asked.

"Just the usual... Do you even know what a reporter does?" she asked.

"Meddle in other people's lives and make trouble for them?" His tone was light. She pulled the shower curtain back to peek out at him. He was bent over the sink washing his face. He was naked and his body looked good, with tan lines on his legs and arms.

He straightened up and she closed the curtain so he

didn't catch her peeking at him. "Ha! No, that's not what I do. Mostly I spend my time doing research and making calls trying to get recalcitrant people to talk to me."

"And if that doesn't work, then you crash their parties."

She shook her head. His easy banter was making her relax. She'd been worrying about what was going on between them, but Conner wasn't treating her any differently than he had before.

"That was only for you," she said. She finished washing her body and though it was an odd-numbered day of the month and normally she didn't wash her hair on those days, she went ahead and did it anyway.

"I'm honored," he said. "Would it bother you if I joined you in the shower?"

She hesitated. She'd been hiding in here so that she wouldn't have to face him, but now she didn't want to anymore.

"Not at all," she said. "In fact, I'm almost finished."

"Good. I'll be quick."

He opened the shower curtain and stepped in. She couldn't resist reaching out to touch him. He gave her a sexy smile.

"I can't make love this morning," she blurted out.

He shook his head. "Okay."

She handed him her loofah and the shower gel and then switched places with him. "I'm going to leave you to it."

"Are you nervous?" he asked.

"Of course not," she said. But she knew she was acting like a ninny. She never let anyone shake her, but Conner was. "I just don't want to tempt you when I know there isn't time to do anything about it."

"I'm always tempted by you," he said, and leaned against her, putting his hand on the wall behind her head and kissing her.

She closed her eyes and tipped her head back. His mouth on hers was soothing and arousing. It made most of her doubts fade away, and she was suddenly very glad that Conner was here with her this morning.

He canted his hips forward and she felt his erection nudge her stomach. Then his hands slid down her body to caress her breasts.

She ran her hands over his wet body as well, finding his hard-on and caressing the entire length of him. He continued kissing her and then put his hands on her waist to lift her off her feet. He leaned back against the wall and she wrapped her arms around his shoulders and her legs around his waist.

"I thought you didn't have time," he said.

"Stop gloating," she said.

She shifted until she felt him poised at the entrance of her body. She slowly took all of him and then rocked her hips against him. He kissed her deeply, driving her on, the tips of her breasts brushing against his chest.

He thrust up into her hard and deep until she felt her orgasm wash over her. She pulled her mouth from his and lowered her head to his shoulder as she felt him jetting his own completion into her body.

She slowly let one leg fall to the floor of the shower. She was dazed by the passion that seemed to flare so effortlessly between them. He pulled himself from her and kissed her softly on the forehead before he gently washed her body and then his own.

She opened the shower curtain and grabbed her towel from the rack, drying off quickly. Then she went back into the bedroom, leaving Conner alone in the bathroom.

She could no longer pretend that last night hadn't changed everything.

* * *

Conner knew she'd been hiding from him in the bathroom. All night long she'd tossed and turned next to him. Neither of them had had a good night's sleep. He knew that, for him, it was second thoughts about what he'd agreed to let her write about him and his family.

But he hadn't made a success out of all his business ventures by backing down once a decision had been made. He'd see it through and manage it so that he was in control.

And that was what this morning had been about for him. Making sure that she didn't have too much time to think about her story. He meant to ensure that she kept her focus on Conner as her lover, not the subject of an interview.

He turned off the shower and realized that he smelled sweet. Glancing down at the bottle of shower gel she'd given him, he groaned when he saw it was "birthday cake"–scented. Damn, he didn't want to walk around all day smelling like this.

He got out of the shower and found a clean towel in the small closet. He dried off and then wrapped it around his waist. He needed a shave and didn't have deodorant or a change of clothes, but that was okay—he'd already sent a text to Randall asking him to pick up those items and bring them over.

The telephone rang and he hesitated for a moment before leaving the bedroom. He heard the muffled sound of Nichole's voice.

When he entered the bedroom, he found Nichole standing in front of her closet with a cordless phone tucked between her shoulder and her ear.

"Yes, Mom, I'm doing fine. I'm sorry I didn't call you last night," she said.

Nichole listened again as she pulled a dark sapphire-blue sheath dress from her closet. She hung it on a hook and then turned, but stopped midstride when she saw him standing there.

"No, I wasn't out on a date. I just went to a dinner party at Jane Macafee's."

She smiled at something her mother said.

"She's just as charming in person as she appears on the show," Nichole said. "I have to go. I'll call you at lunchtime."

Nichole listened again.

"Love you, too."

She hung up the phone and tossed it onto the bed. It seemed to Conner that she and her mother had a really good relationship. But how could that be, based on her past?

"My mom calls me if I don't talk to her every day. Even though I've been living here for more than ten years, she's still afraid something bad will happen to me," Nichole said.

"My mom is the same way," Conner said. "She pretends she's calling to ask me about business or other things but she manages to talk to me every day."

She walked over to her dresser and pulled out a matching bra-and-panty set. This one was cream-colored and had a lace trim on the edge. He knew he should be getting dressed as well, but he enjoyed the intimacy of watching Nichole slowly clothe herself.

"Are you going to keep staring at me?" she asked.

"I can't help myself. You're gorgeous," he said.

She gave a quick curtsy. "I'm so glad you think so."

She was funny and quirky and every second he spent with her made him want more.

And that made her dangerous.

Who would have thought that this woman would be able to rock his world the way she had? He was used to dealing with powerful, beautiful women, but Nichole was different.

She dressed quickly and he went over to his own clothes and began putting them on. When she was seated at her vanity table, he glanced over at her and noticed that she had been watching him in the mirror.

She quickly picked up a makeup brush and drew it across her face, refusing to meet his eyes in the mirror. He understood that she was a complicated woman and that no matter how much she'd enjoyed the sex with him, there were bound to be some heavy emotions inside her this morning.

"Are you okay?" he asked, thinking he probably sounded pretty inane. "I guess we can see that I'm definitely not a reporter given my lame questions."

She gave him a sad half smile. "That's for sure. And I'm fine. A little tired."

"Tired sounds like an excuse," he said as he buttoned his shirt. "Do you regret last night?"

She shook her head. "Not at all. Since the first moment we talked at the Fourth of July party, I've thought of nothing else but getting you into my bed."

"Me, too. But that doesn't mean that this morning you might feel differently. When I was first starting out in business, I set all these financial goals for myself and in my mind I thought once I have this amount of money I'll feel secure. But the truth was the money didn't make a difference."

She turned on her vanity stool to face him. "What did make the difference?"

"A sense of confidence in myself. I had to trust that I would continue making the right decisions and that I didn't need to stop at one good deal to ensure the future."

She nodded. He'd told her something personal that he hadn't meant to. Dammit, he needed to be more on his guard around her. And this wasn't even her fault. He had to watch himself because she mattered to him.

He suddenly realized that he cared about her and not in the general way he'd thought he had. She mattered to him. Her happiness mattered to him.

"Thank you for sharing that," she said.

"You're welcome." He finished dressing quickly. Now he was the one who felt awkward and that wasn't like him. His cell phone beeped and he glanced down at the screen to see he had a text from Randall saying he was waiting downstairs.

"I'm going to get out of here. Are you free for lunch or drinks tonight?"

"Lunch would be better. I have to drop by the set of *Sexy & Single*."

"Lunch it is—does the Big Apple Kiwi Klub at noon work for you?" he asked. "We can discuss the details of your moving in with me then."

She nodded.

He stood up and walked over to her, pulled her into his arms and kissed her softly. "Have a good day, red."

Then he turned and walked out of her bedroom, but he knew he couldn't walk away from the new emotions that were flowing inside of him.

Nichole's morning flew by. Her editorial meeting was long and boring as usual, but she was preoccupied with thoughts of Conner and the previous night. A couple of her coworkers mentioned that she seemed distracted and she told them that she was on a new story and that was all that was on her mind.

But part of her knew that Conner was definitely a distraction. She'd always been 100 percent focused at work and today she wasn't. Instead, she remembered the way he'd felt inside her this morning in her shower. And she hoped that tonight she'd sleep a little better, but doubted it.

She was his mistress now. She didn't know what the reality of that would entail, but she did know that there was going to be a lot more of Conner in her life. And she had to get it together to focus on the story she wanted to write or else she was going to find that she'd wasted this time with him.

But part of her just wanted to revel in being in a new relationship. That scared her. Especially since Conner had made it clear that he was moving on when their month of being lovers was up.

She glanced at her iPhone and saw that she had fifteen minutes to get across town to meet Conner for lunch. She wanted to be prepared to ask him a few interview questions or at least schedule some interview time so that she didn't get distracted by being his lover.

Just as she was about to walk out of the office, her phone rang. She glanced at the caller ID and saw that it was Gail.

"Hey, girl," she said, forcing herself to sound cheerful, even though she was in the midst of her greatest moral dilemma ever.

"Hey. Are you free for lunch today? I wanted to talk to you and see how things were going," Gail said.

"I can't. Why do you want to talk to me?"

"You seemed a little…*lost* is the wrong word, so don't get mad, but just unsettled about the entire thing with Conner Macafee," Gail said.

"I *am* lost," Nichole admitted. "But only because he's not like other guys and I don't know exactly what to do to handle him. I could use a sounding board."

"I thought so. I'm busy tonight, but I can do breakfast or lunch tomorrow," Gail said.

"Maybe breakfast. I'm supposed to drop by the set of

the TV show tomorrow, so if you tag along maybe we can rope Willow into joining us."

"I'm already on it," Gail said. "I'll text you the details later. Bye."

"Gail?"

"Yes?"

"Thanks for calling," Nichole said. She knew that she wasn't comfortable reaching out to her friends because she never wanted them to think she was whiney, but she needed someone to talk to.

"No problem. You and Willow are my soul sisters and we have to look out for each other."

"I know that, but it's hard when we're all so busy."

"I'm never too busy for you," Gail said. "Take care, honey."

"You, too."

Nichole felt less alone when she hung up the phone. She left her office and hailed a cab. Traffic was heavy and she sent a text to Conner that she'd be ten minutes late. He replied right away.

I'm running late, too.

I'll get a table if I'm there first.

I have one reserved. See you soon.

Nichole was unsure if she should answer back. She knew it would just be something like *okay*, but she hated to not respond to a message. When she IMed with Gail and Willow, they teased her that she had to have the last word. And she knew it was true. Finally, she just texted back *Okay* and put her phone away.

The cab pulled to a stop in front of the Big Apple Kiwi

Klub, which housed a hotel and nightclub in one facility. The hotel had a Michelin-starred restaurant and featured a traveling exhibit of Gustav Klimt's work. The Klubs were an international chain, owned by Gail's fiancé, Russell Holloway.

Nichole exited the taxi and headed to the restaurant on the third floor. She gave Conner's name to the maître d' and by the time their table was ready, Conner had arrived. He put his hand on the small of her back as they followed the seating hostess to their table.

No one looking at them would think that they weren't involved. Nichole realized that she needed to have a chat with her editor and let him know that she was "dating" Conner before the story ran so that it didn't look like anything inappropriate was going on.

That was just another complication to this deal she'd made. She knew the stakes were high and she'd gambled everything on this being a story that could take her career to the next level.

Once they were seated, she noticed that Conner had found time to shave and change his clothes after he'd left her apartment this morning.

He ordered sparkling water for both of them and told the waiter they'd signal him when they were ready to order. "We need a few minutes to talk."

"No problem, sir," the waiter said and backed away.

"I hope you don't mind, but I wanted to talk to you before we order our food."

"Not at all. What's up?" she asked.

"I wanted to give you a chance to back out of our bargain," he said.

"Why now?" she asked.

"It seems as if it's weighing heavily on your mind and I don't want you to feel that you have to continue on with it."

"Will you still sit down for an interview?" she asked.

He shook his head. She felt angry that *he* might want to renege on their deal now that she'd slept with him. "I'm not going back on my word, Conner. Are you?"

Ten

Conner immediately realized his mistake, but he had wanted to give her a chance to back out. "I didn't mean it at all the way you've taken it."

"How did you mean it, then?"

"Just that I can tell how much our bargain is troubling you…and I wanted to give you an out."

"I appreciate that, but I'd only take it if you still intended to pursue a relationship with me as well as letting me talk to you about Matchmakers, Inc."

"I understand. Let's put my question behind us. Shall we order lunch and then discuss the details of our arrangement?"

She nodded, but there was a tightness to her features that told him he wasn't forgiven. And he couldn't blame her. He'd worded his idea in the worst possible way.

And he'd forgotten something extremely important: She'd slept with him last night and undoubtedly felt a little vulnerable as far as he was concerned this morning.

They both ordered and once they were alone again, Nichole pulled a notebook from her purse and a fountain pen. "I would like to get a couple of interviews scheduled."

"I understand. I think for both our sakes, maybe we should draw up an agreement between the two of us."

"Like what?"

"Just what I expect from you and what you expect from me," he said.

She wrote their names next to each other on a blank page in her notebook then drew a line down the middle. Under her name she wrote the word *mistress* and under his *interviews*.

"That's just the start," she said. "We agreed last night that you would do an interview about the matchmaking service and that you would allow me to observe you with your family."

"Yes, we did," he said.

She added those to the column under his name.

"*Mistress* is a vague term," he said. "But I'd like you to live with me in my apartment for the duration of our time together."

"I don't know about that. Will you allow me to check with my boss this afternoon?" she asked. "I'm going to say simply that I've interviewed you and we are dating. Let him know about the relationship and make sure that he's cool with it."

"Shouldn't you have already checked?" he asked. It sounded like there were details she hadn't covered and that didn't seem like Nichole.

"I have to check it out. There are other reporters who have written about their significant others, but I just want to let my editor know we are dating. If we hadn't been seen out in public together we might have a chance at remaining under the radar, but I'd rather not take any additional chances."

"Agreed," he said. "Barring any problems with that, I think you should move into my apartment this evening."

"Isn't that quick?" she asked.

"It's a little late to think of that now. You're mine, red, and I want you under my roof."

She shivered with sensual excitement at the way he claimed her. Her mind tried to warn her not to let it go to her head, though. She had to focus on the interview. That should help her keep cool as far as he was concerned. Not so easily agitated by everything he said and did.

"Sounds good. Do you have time to meet with me tomorrow for the interview?" she asked.

He pulled out his iPhone and after a few minutes said, "I can give you thirty minutes tomorrow."

"That's not enough time, but it will do for a start. When?" she asked.

"Ten-thirty," he said.

She jotted that under the column for his name.

"I'd like to do one interview at the Matchmakers, Inc. offices," she said. "Do you keep an office there?"

"I don't. I'm not all that involved with the everyday operations of the company."

"Do you ever go down there?"

"Occasionally, for board meetings. We can use the boardroom at Macafee International if you don't feel like using my office," he said. "Are you afraid of a repeat of what happened last time?"

She was. But then they could be riding together in a cab and she'd want him. What was the hold he had over her? If past experience had taught her anything, once she'd slept with a man usually the lust started to wane, but the opposite was true with Conner.

She seemed to want him more. Even now, sitting across from him and writing down details of their indecent agreement, she was thinking about the way his hands had caressed her body last night and the way his mouth felt against hers when he kissed her.

"Not unless you are," she said, leaning forward and taking his hand in hers.

"Hell, I'm not afraid it will happen—I'm counting on it," he said.

She almost smiled, but Conner was too self-confident to begin with. She didn't need to react to everything he said and let him know that she was under his spell.

Damn. She hadn't thought about it that way before, but that was the truth. She was truly under his spell. No other man had made her feel this way. Which was why she'd been a serial dater with her little boy toys.

But now, as she sat across from Conner and stared into his blue eyes, she realized that she wanted so much more from him. She wanted something that felt scary. Something she'd never tried before.

She wanted something permanent and solid. And she knew that she had no idea how to make that work. It was a good thing she was writing down the details of this arrangement because maybe seeing those stark facts would help her remember that Conner was just a story and she was his mistress, not his girlfriend. He had been very clear on what he wanted from her and that was sex—not forever.

Forever had never been that important to her because, after her childhood, she'd always believed that it would be smart for her to live alone. But there was something about Conner that made her rethink that. Or maybe it was all the stories she'd been doing on matchmaking. She was forgetting the realistic woman she'd always been and dreaming of things she wasn't sure she wanted.

* * *

Conner had booked the lunch right before another meeting so he wouldn't be tempted to linger too long with Nichole. When his iPhone beeped to remind him it was time to go, he signaled for the check.

"Text me as soon as you find out from your boss if you can move in with me. From my side that is one of my must-haves."

"You made that clear. I'll let you know as soon as I can," she said.

"I have a meeting in fifteen minutes," Conner said as he handed his credit card to the waiter. "I'm sorry we didn't get to finish talking over the details, but I feel as if we got the main things out and on the table."

"I do, too," she said.

"Great. I'll be looking forward to hearing from you about tonight."

"Not a problem," she said, closing the notebook and putting it in her purse.

Conner signed the check, then stood up and followed Nichole from the dining room. He was very aware that most of the men in the room watched her as she walked. She was one of those women who drew men's gazes. Conner felt a spark of jealousy and reached out to grab her hand. She glanced up at him.

"What's the matter?"

"Nothing. I just wanted to make sure that every man in the room knows you're with me," he said.

"I guess I should be glad you didn't pull me into your arms and kiss me," she said.

"I thought about it. But one kiss is never enough with you and me," he said.

She shook her head. "You're very arrogant, you know that, right?"

"I'm not being arrogant," he said. "I'm being posses-
sive. You're mine by our agreement."

"I know," she said.

As soon as they exited the restaurant, he did drop a light
kiss on her lips, but then quickly stepped away.

"I knew you wouldn't be able to resist," she said.

He arched one eyebrow at her.

"Me. I have a power over you," she said.

"You do? We can talk about this power tonight," he said.

"Yes, we can," she agreed. "I have a lot of things I want
to talk to you about."

"I'll bet you do," he said.

The elevator arrived and they both got in and rode it
to the ground floor. Once they stepped outside the lobby,
Conner saw his car waiting. "Do you want me to have
Randall take you back to your office after he drops me at
my meeting?"

"No, thanks. I'll take a cab," she said.

He couldn't resist kissing her again and for that very
reason almost didn't do it, but he was in control of this arrangement and his own body. So he kissed her to prove to
himself that he could stop if he wanted to.

"Until tonight."

He got in the back of the waiting Rolls Royce Phantom
and glanced back only once as Randall drove away. He
saw Nichole standing there with her hand on her mouth
watching his car. Then she shook her head and turned and
started walking in the opposite direction.

His cell phone rang and he glanced at the caller ID. It
was his mom. Probably the last person he should be talking to right now when he was feeling…not any particular
thing, just feeling emotions. For so long he'd pretended that
he was aloof and didn't feel the same way other people did.

Often he felt superior by his ability to keep his emotions out of his daily life. But he knew now that it was only the fact that he'd never met a woman like Nichole before. She tempted him in ways that had nothing to do with sex.

He answered the call. "Hi, Mom."

"Are you busy, Conner?" she asked.

Even though he'd told her he wouldn't answer if he couldn't talk, she always asked him that. "No. What's up?"

"I'm having a charity open house in Bridgehampton this weekend and I want you to come."

"What day?"

"Saturday, but I was thinking you could come down Friday night and stay until Sunday and you can bring that reporter you had dinner with at your sister's house the other night."

"How do you know about that?"

"Janey. She doesn't mind talking to me every day."

He was annoyed with his sister for telling their mom about Nichole. "Did she mention she's dating Palmer?"

"Is she? No, she didn't. I guess I'll include him in my weekend invitation, too. Oh, this will be so nice. Both of you home and with—"

"Mom, I will come to the event on Saturday but I can't make it for the entire weekend."

"Oh, really?"

"Yes, is there anything else?"

"Jane said you and Nichole Reynolds really hit it off. Did you?"

"Yes, we did. But it's not serious," he said.

"It never is with you," she said with a forlorn sigh. "I would like grandkids one day."

"Janey can give them to you, too," Conner said.

"I think she's waiting for a sign from you that life is okay," his mom said.

That couldn't be true. "I don't see why. She's better at making a home than I ever was."

"You both have created what you felt was missing when everything happened with your father. You created financial security for all of us and Janey the perfect house. But it's not enough, and I don't know what to do to show you both that."

Conner didn't like hearing what his mom had to say. He knew that he put money first and had made interpersonal relationships a distant second. He hadn't gotten to be thirty-five by not knowing what made him tick, but it hurt to hear his mom sum it up that way.

"I'll be there on Saturday," he said. "And I will be bringing Nichole Reynolds. I've got to go now, Mom. Love you."

He hung up before she could say anything more. After the lunch with Nichole, the last thing he needed was an emotional discussion with his mom. He wasn't sure how it had happened, but his tidy little life had suddenly been thrown upside down. Actually, he did know how it had happened and exactly who was to blame—Nichole Reynolds.

Nichole had taken the subway back to her office, hoping that by being around other people she'd be less likely to get stuck in her own head. But it didn't work. She was still unsure of what she'd agreed to with Conner and the more time she spent thinking about it, the worse that knot of tension in her stomach became.

She had had a number of uncomfortable conversations with people over the years. She had gotten to be such a good reporter by asking tough questions, but she'd never had to discuss her personal life with her boss before and she knew she was going to have to do that today.

She had the distinct feeling that her own knowledge of

what she'd agreed to with Conner was coloring her feelings on the issue, but she couldn't help that.

She took the stairs up to her floor instead of the elevator, no doubt to put off the inevitable. But as luck would have it, her boss was in his office when she stopped by to see him.

"Do you have a minute?" she asked.

"I've got a few. What do you need?" he asked.

She stepped into his office and closed the door behind her. Ross Kleeman had started as reporter a long time ago and he'd managed to keep *America Today* vibrant and profitable. Many newspapers hadn't made the transition to the web-based editions as skillfully as *America Today*, thanks in large part to Ross.

"Well, two things. The first is that I got an interview with Conner Macafee. I see this as a two-part story. The first will focus on his matchmaking company, featured in the new *Sexy & Single* television show. And the second will be a color piece on how the scandal with his father influenced his business and personal choices."

"Wow. How'd you get him to agree to that? And what do you mean by color piece?" Ross asked.

"How I got him to agree kind of ties into the second thing I wanted to tell you—Conner and I are dating. Is that going to be a problem?"

Ross leaned back in his chair and crossed his arms over his chest. "We can disclose your relationship when we print the articles. That should take care of any ethics issues. So he agreed to let you write about that because you're dating?"

Nichole nodded. "For the second piece, I'm going to rely on my own observations, since he won't talk to me about the scandal with his father. But I can see how it has influenced the choices that Conner has made. To some extent I can see that in his sister, too."

"Interesting. Depending on the type of story you end up writing, we might be able to run it in the *Weekend Magazine* edition."

"Okay. I don't intend it to be an exposé. It'll be a longer version of my usual column," she said.

"See what you come up with. And think feature piece instead of column when you're writing," Ross said. "Was that all?"

"Yes," she said, heading out of his office.

She walked back to her cubicle and stowed her purse in her desk while turning on her computer. She got out her cell phone to text Conner.

No problems with my boss. I can move in tonight.

A few minutes passed before she got a reply.

Good. I have a 5 pm meeting so I can't meet you until 8. Will call when I'm done here.

OK

Do you have to get the last word in all the time?

Yes. ☺

OK

TTYL

You win.

Good.

There was no other response from Conner and Nichole smiled to herself. That was the part that always surprised her about him. He was fun. He shouldn't be because he was arrogant and too used to getting his own way. But he made her smile a lot of the time.

Part of her was worried about how she was going to be able to manage to live with him and not fall in love with him. It was bad enough that they had this bargain. She wished she could keep her emotions out of it.

She wondered what other men's mistresses did. When she was in college, she'd done an article on a study that was conducted at NYU on brain chemistry and sex, and she knew that no matter how sophisticated society was, at its most basic level everyone was still programmed to find a mate and procreate.

If she tried, maybe she could use science to protect herself, but she doubted it. Conner just didn't fit in the nice little mold she'd always used to make sure that she didn't fall in love with anyone.

What she needed to do was somehow figure out how to make every time they were together about the articles she was writing instead of their attraction.

But she knew it would be next to impossible because she wanted him.

It hadn't taken much prodding on her part to get him to kiss her after lunch. She'd needed it. She needed to know that she wasn't the only one who was helpless in this infatuation. Conner seemed so much in control—both of himself and the world around him. Something she'd always assumed she was, but he put those beliefs to shame.

Her career had only been so super-important to her because the men she'd dated in the past had been boys. She hadn't realized that the fun she was having had been designed to shield her commitment until this moment.

She put her head in her hands and stared at her desktop. In her mind's eye she saw the list she'd written at lunch with Conner and she knew that she'd left one very important thing out of her column.

Don't fall for Conner.

He'd told her he didn't want to hurt her, and he'd been honest from the beginning, so she knew if she did get hurt she'd have no one to blame but herself. But that still didn't help her figure out how she was going to get her story, be his mistress and not fall in love with him.

Eleven

Conner had expected Nichole to need more time or try to make up some reason why she couldn't move in with him, but she seemed determined to live up to the bargain she'd struck with him.

His respect for her grew a little bit as he realized that. The more he knew about her as a person, the less fearful he was of anything she'd print about him. But that was a foolish way of thinking. He had to remember that she was here for a story and he was going to make sure that she got the information he allowed her to have and nothing more.

His apartment was a penthouse in a building on the Upper East Side. It ran the entire length of the building and had a glass wall overlooking his patio. He'd spent a lot of money on decorating and it felt like home when he opened the door.

Conner ushered Nichole into his apartment. He was carrying her small overnight bag, leaving her with her computer and purse. Randall was bringing up the rest of her bags, but overall, she hadn't brought a lot of stuff.

"Welcome to my home," he said as they walked over the threshold and into the big open-plan living room.

"Thank you. I had to tell my parents I was staying with a friend while my building had some work done," she said, blurting it out. "My mom calls on my house phone all the time."

Her demeanor was the only clue that she was at all nervous about moving in with him. As she looked around his apartment, he tried to see it through her eyes. He knew it was stylish and well decorated, but he wondered what she thought of it.

"Okay, do you want to give them my home phone number as well?"

"Yes, if you don't mind. That will make both of them feel better. I don't want them to know about you, though," she said.

"What do you mean?"

"If they know that I'm living with you, they'll want to meet you and then, when we break up in a month, they'll be disappointed for me and for themselves and the grandchildren they are dying to have."

"My mom is a little bit like that, too."

"So you can sympathize," she said.

"I'm going to give you your own bedroom so that you can have some privacy. I know you were worried that my insistence that you live here might have taken that from you."

She nodded. "Thank you. I actually do a lot of my writing at home because our office is so noisy."

He led her to a large guest bedroom that was next to the master bedroom. "This room has a desk in it. We can bring the one from your apartment over, if you'd prefer that."

"This will be fine," she said.

He put her bag on the bed and then stood there for a minute. He'd never had a mistress before. He had some image in his head of himself as a sheikh and her as his harem girl, but he knew better than to tell her to get naked.

"I'll leave you to settle in," he said. "Have you had dinner?"

"No," she said. "My day was busier than I expected it to be."

"I haven't, either. Would you like to join me on the patio in twenty minutes? My housekeeper left dinner waiting for us."

"Yes, I would."

He walked out of the room before he gave in to his instincts and swept her into his arms and onto the bed. He had thought about this moment all day long. What he would do once he had her here in his home. He had decided he'd keep her off balance. But he hadn't counted on her keeping him off balance as well.

He went to his own bedroom and changed from his suit into a pair of khaki shorts and a plain black T-shirt. He reviewed his email on his cell phone and responded to the urgent ones. Then sitting back in the wingback chair next to his bed, he realized that he was excited that Nichole was here.

Sometimes when he was here, he felt alone. He'd never invited anyone to spend the night here before and having a companion appealed to him. The only trepidation he felt was that he had to be on guard not to say anything detrimental she could use in her articles.

There was a knock on his door and he pocketed his cell phone as he went to open it. Nichole stood there in a pair of skintight jeans and a tank top. Her feet were bare and she'd pulled her hair up into a high ponytail.

"So this is your room?" she asked, brushing past him to enter.

"Yes," he said. He couldn't take his eyes off her as she walked around his room. He'd intended for sex to be the thing that kept her from asking him too many questions, but he hadn't thought that she could distract him in the same way.

She walked over to the walnut dresser and ran her finger along its polished surface. There was a small watch box on the surface and a picture of his mom and sister from the previous Christmas. Otherwise, the room was devoid of personal mementoes.

"Kind of sterile, isn't it?" she asked.

"I don't like clutter," he said. "Especially in here. What did you expect to find?"

"Some clues to the real Conner Macafee."

"You'll find more 'clues' to him in bed, red."

"Why do you call me that?"

"I don't know. You're fiery and full of passion. It suits you."

She nodded. "I hated my red hair growing up," she admitted.

"I hated that everyone thought they knew me growing up," he said.

"I'll bet you did. Did you go to a private school?"

"Yes, it was very exclusive. Lots of old-money families. We were pretty much from the same type of background. And our families mostly knew each other."

"But you were different than the other kids?" she asked.

"I thought so, but then I'll bet we all did. It's hard to be a rebel when you have everything," he said.

"But I'll bet when you suddenly lost it all it was much easier," she said.

"You could say that. Let's go to the kitchen. I have a feeling I'm going to need a drink."

Nichole followed him to the kitchen, looking around his apartment along the way. It wasn't sterile, and she realized she shouldn't have said his bedroom was. It was just that he didn't have a lot photos on the walls. He had artwork, though.

"I guess rich people put up artwork instead of personal photos?"

"I don't know. I just put up what I like. My mom and my sister are the only two people I'm close to," he said, going to the chrome refrigerator. "Want a Corona?"

"Yes, please," she said.

"Have a seat," he said, gesturing to the bar area.

She hopped up on one of the stools and noticed that his kitchen was state of the art, with a professional-grade cooktop. "Do you cook?"

"No, but I have a personal chef I use for dinner parties and events I hold here. She insisted that the kitchen must be like this. Mainly I use the microwave to heat things up following Mrs. Plumb's instructions."

"I use my microwave a lot, too. I just don't have the time to cook at home," she said, taking the Corona from him when he handed it to her with a wedge of lime in the top. She pushed the lime into the bottle and then took a swallow of the beer.

"Is Jane the chef you use?"

"Yes, she is," Conner said, coming over to lean against the counter across from her.

"Why didn't you just use her name?" she asked.

"I'm used to never talking about her."

She had known Conner was going to be a tough interview, but she hadn't realized how much he kept up his guard. If he was never going to let her in, how the hell was she going to get the information she needed?

"It's okay to use her name with me," Nichole said.

"I know that. Force of habit," Conner said. He took a long swallow of his beer and then set the bottle on the countertop. "Let's see what we have for dinner."

He opened the bottom warming oven, bending down to see what was inside. She enjoyed the view of his backside and gave a little wolf whistle to let him know. She didn't want Conner to feel pressured to answer her questions and she knew the only way to make sure he didn't was to (1) keep him off guard and (2) keep things light. He expected her to go for the hard questions and she would. But not at first.

"Like the view?" he asked, shaking his hips.

"Yes, I do. So what's on the menu other than you?" she asked.

"Salmon en croute. Mrs. Plumb has been experimenting with some different recipes lately."

"Sounds good. How long has Mrs. Plumb worked for you?"

"Eight years. I've lived here that long, too," he said. Using oven mitts, he removed two dishes from the oven and set them on the countertop.

"Can you carry both our beers?"

"Yes, sir," she said.

He led the way to the glass door with the automatic sensor that opened it when he approached. Once they were outside, he set the plates on the table, which was already set with glasses, napkins and flatware.

"I like that door," she said. "Very high tech."

"I like convenience and I have the money to get what I want," he said. "Be right back."

She set the beers down at each of their spots and then

took a seat and waited for him to come. He returned with two salad plates, setting one next to her dish and one at his place.

"I probably should serve wine with this, but I don't care for it."

"Any wine?" she asked.

"Not really. I'll drink it at dinner parties because it's expected, but when I'm at home I don't touch it."

"I really love a dry wine, but mainly I drink it with my girlfriends when we're hanging out."

"You mentioned that Jane was good friends with Willow and Willow is one of your friends?"

"Yes. Willow and Gail Little and I all grew up together," Nichole said. "We all ended up going to college in New York and just have grown closer over the years. It's really nice having them here with me. It makes me feel like I've got a little bit of home close by."

"I have some good friends, but they are mainly business associates who have the same hobbies I do," Conner said.

Nichole relaxed as dinner progressed and noticed that Conner did, too. It was almost like any other first date, except that they both knew they'd sleep together tonight.

"What are your hobbies?" she asked.

"Sailing," he said. "I love being out on my yacht."

"What do you like about it?" She suspected it probably had a lot to do with the fact that when he was out there no one could bother him.

He shrugged and took a bite of his dinner. She watched him chew and then realized that she was fascinated by everything about this man.

"I guess the solitude. There's usually poor cell phone reception so no one can reach me from the office. I tend to go out alone or with a very small crew so no one bothers me."

She could see why that would appeal to him. Conner

had been shaped into the man he was today by a very intrusive incident in his past. He'd always need to be alone to feel safe.

Maybe that was why he wanted her as his mistress instead of his girlfriend. Maybe that added layer gave him the security of knowing that he'd still have the assurance of being alone when their time together ended.

She knew there was no maybe about it. That was exactly why he'd set it up the way he had. But what did it say about her that she'd agreed to his terms?

She knew she wanted her career to continue to be her focus, but having met Conner, she doubted it would satisfy her the way that he did. Oh, that wasn't right. It was more the way she imagined he would fill her life if she let herself really care for him.

He made her want things that she didn't think she ever would. And no matter how hard she tried to switch back to the way she'd been before, she knew she couldn't. Something inside her had been irrevocably changed by Conner Macafee. That should bother her. Strangely, it didn't.

Conner enjoyed the evening with Nichole. But it felt homey in a way and that bothered him a lot. He didn't want to feel too comfortable with her.

Turned on by her, of course, but comfortable, no way. He needed to keep his edge and his wits about him. She'd thrown him with her casual sexiness and it was time for him to start regaining the ground he'd lost earlier.

She'd asked him questions, but he tried to keep them on even footing by learning just as much about her. Nichole was a mystery to him and each new thing he uncovered only brought more questions. She had a natural elegance to all her moves and she was funny and had a sharp wit.

She was giving him the rundown on the person who

sat behind her at work. A sportswriter who, in Nichole's words, spent most of his time trying to relive his glory days. "The thing is, he's a great guy and a terrific writer. If he didn't talk so much about his failed career in baseball, people would like him. He should be more like Jack Crown."

"In what way?" Conner asked as he made coffee for them both.

"Jack doesn't dwell on the fact that he didn't have the career playing pro football that he should have had. He just lives in the now."

"I see what you mean. That's why I don't like to talk about my past. What's important is what's happening now," Conner said.

She gave him a sardonic look. "Your past influences everything you do today. Being a jock in high school and telling everyone about how you were the reason your team won the state championship is a totally different story."

He shook his head as he added cream and sugar to his coffee and just cream to hers. "It's only different because you want to know about my past. If I was Joe Schmoe and you'd never heard of my dad, you wouldn't care what went on."

"Fair enough, but you're not. So that point is moot," she said, taking her cup from him. "I was very excited to see you have a Keurig machine. I love mine and almost packed it."

"Why?"

"I need coffee and lots of it."

"Doesn't it leave you wired?" he asked, sitting next to her at the counter.

"Not really. I just love the taste," she said, then shook her head at him. "I don't know why I'm going on about coffee. It's really not that big a deal."

"You're cute when you let your guard down," he said.

"Is that what I'm doing?" she asked.

"I think so. I think you've decided the only way to get me to open up is to open up yourself," he said.

"You're a shrewd man, Mr. Macafee, but I'm not going to let you manipulate me," she said. "I could tell from the moment we met that you were too used to getting your own way."

He laughed. "I wouldn't dream of manipulating you. And we all want our own way so of course I'm used to it. I've worked very hard to make sure things happen the way I want them to."

He had spent years designing his life for the best possible outcome. It was no easy task to get to where he was and keep everyone in the world from asking about the one thing they all wanted to know. He'd never fully escaped the salaciousness of his father's scandal. Yet he'd moved through life ignoring the questions and keeping reporters at bay.

How then did he come to have Nichole sitting next to him? He still wasn't clear about that. He'd thought that the reasons he'd given himself were honest.

He had wanted her and here she was.

"Ready to see the rest of the place?" he asked.

"Sure," she said. "Why didn't you move to the West Coast after everything happened with your dad?"

"Mom said it would be too much like running away— like we had something to hide," he said.

"Your mom sounds like a very strong woman. And so is your sister," she said.

"You're a strong woman, too," he said. "I'm used to women who know what they want and aren't afraid to go after it."

He led her up the stairs set to the left of the hallway that led to the bedrooms. "This is my play area."

"I can't wait to see what's up here."

There was a full-sized pool table and a media center. Built onto the other wall was a bar with six barstools and behind it was a fully stocked liquor cabinet. He led her past the game room into a large study. There was a dark wood desk that sat in front of a large plate-glass window. On either side of it were floor-to-ceiling bookcases. The shelves were overflowing with books.

She walked over to the bookshelves and took her time reading the titles. There were some classics and of course there were the business books, but she was surprised to see books by Machiavelli and the Baroness Orczy.

"The Scarlet Pimpernel."

"I was young when I read it. It was my mother's favorite. She told me he was the first Batman."

Nichole had to laugh at that. "Your mother sounds like she's a lot of fun."

Conner had a quiet look on his face. "She's the best. She's always just let me and Jane do what we wanted, but kept us in line at the same time. She's a good parent."

"Are you glad you live so close to her?"

"Yes. Jane and I take turns keeping an eye on her, but she doesn't need the attention."

"What kind of work do you do from home?" she asked.

"Whatever needs doing," he said. "If you weren't here I would have eaten at my desk and answered emails until eleven."

"Workaholic!"

"Yes, I am. But it's impossible to have a successful business and not be. Everyone talks about wanting to have balance, but it takes drive and ambition to be successful and that type of personality doesn't want to spend weeks having downtime."

That said a lot about Conner and she added it to the image of him she was building in her head to write her article. He might have been born with a silver spoon in his mouth, but there was nothing lazy about him. He didn't expect anything to be handed to him and she admired him for it.

"Ready to go downstairs and see the rest of the rooms?" he asked.

"No, but I am ready to see your bedroom again," she said.

He took her hand and led her downstairs to his bedroom, where he made love to her and she stopped thinking about stories and bargains and just enjoyed being in her lover's arms until he carried her back to her own bed in the middle of the night and she was reminded of those very facts.

Twelve

Nichole woke early, showered and left Conner's apartment without seeing him. Unfortunately, once she'd left it was too early for her to meet Gail and Willow for breakfast. But she knew if she stayed she'd feel pushed into saying or doing something with Conner that she shouldn't.

Last night she'd been ballsy and acted like being his mistress was all part of her plan, but being carried back to her bed after she'd fallen asleep wasn't cool, no matter how she tried to make it work in her head. She'd thought she'd been prepared for the reality of being his mistress, but she hadn't been.

She knew that it was past time for her romantic dreams about Conner to be put to bed, but it wasn't that easy. She felt as if she'd won some things from him the night before. He'd answered her questions. Granted, they'd been easy ones, but still.

And this morning, having gotten absolutely no sleep,

she was feeling very emotional. She stopped at Starbucks for a coffee and texted both Willow and Gail to see what time they were meeting. She quickly heard back that if she and Gail were willing to go to Brooklyn, Willow could meet in thirty minutes.

Nichole texted back that worked for her and hailed a cab to get out of Manhattan. They met at a coffee shop that served what Willow called the best breakfast burrito in New York. Gail had to cancel so it was just the two of them.

"Okay, what's up with you? You never can meet this early," Willow said after the waiter had set down their food and coffee.

Nichole might be making her living as a reporter, but she was uncomfortable being the one on the other side of the questions. She knew what she wanted to say to her friend, but not how to say it. Finally, she just took a deep breath and blurted out, "I've agreed to be Conner's mistress in exchange for interviewing him."

Willow stopped midchew and just looked at her incredulously, which made Nichole realize she should have chosen some different words, maybe something that made it sound a little less like what it was.

Willow finished chewing the bite she had in her mouth and then reached across the table to take Nichole's hand. "Okay, first of all why?"

"He wouldn't agree to be interviewed otherwise."

"So he's a pig?" Willow asked.

"No. It's not like that. You know…actually you might not know this, but after he kept avoiding me on the set and refused to take my calls, I crashed his family's Fourth of July party and when he confronted me…well, we had chemistry."

"Okay, this is making more sense now. So he wanted

you and you, being a good little reporter, said no, my story comes first."

"Yes, Willow, it was very *Perils of Pauline* with my swooning and putting my hand on my forehead," Nichole said, getting a little frustrated with her friend.

"I'm sorry," Willow said. "But this is only a problem because…I'm not sure why. How is being his mistress any different than those one-night stands you've had or your vacation boyfriends?"

"It's different because I like him," Nichole said.

"And that's the heart of the matter. You've always been careful to keep men at arm's length and it was easy for you because you picked men who weren't looking for anything serious."

"Conner definitely isn't looking for anything serious. Do you think that's why I like him? The challenge?" Nichole asked. She desperately wanted to figure this out, so she could just go back to how she used to be.

"Maybe, but it's more likely, given the chemistry you said the two of you have, that you've found a real man you're interested in," Willow said.

"That's what I was afraid of. What am I going to do, Will?"

"I guess backing out is not an option," her friend said.

"No. I want that interview. Ross is talking about putting the story in the *Weekend Magazine* edition if it's good enough. You know how long I've waited for that?"

"I do," Willow said. "Well, then, the only solution is to keep things light. See if pretending he's one of your boys—"

"Please stop calling them that. There weren't that many of them and they were men," Nichole said.

"Okay, I guess I was always jealous of your little hotties," Willow admitted.

"You can be jealous," Nichole said with a small laugh.

The conversation drifted to breakfast, which they both started eating, and they finished their meal with gossip about the latest couple on *Sexy & Single*. "Rikki finally lightened up as far as Paul is concerned. I think when you drop by the set this week, you're going to see a different woman."

"What did he do?"

"That's the million-dollar question," Willow said. "It happened off camera, but the ice queen has started to thaw."

The waiter gave them the check and as they both put cash on the table to cover their portion of the bill, Willow glanced over at Nichole.

"Are you going to be okay?"

Nichole didn't know the answer to that. She knew that she had to be because, as her father had said more than once, "Life goes on whether we're ready for it or not." But she had never felt as hurt by any other person in her adult life as she had last night when Conner had dropped her in her bed and left the room.

"I don't know."

"I'm here if you need to talk more," Willow said as they stood up. Willow hugged her and Nichole was grateful for her friend.

"Thanks."

"Nic?"

"Yes?"

"There will be other interviews," Willow said. "If you don't think it's right for you personally, I'd bail and just chalk this one up to experience."

Nichole nodded and held her hand up for a cab as they walked outside. "I will. But I'm not a quitter."

"No, you're not, but that's not always a good thing. You

can't keep at something that isn't any good for you. Just remember that you deserve to be successful and happy."

The cab arrived and those words echoed in her head all the way back to her office. She knew that a lot of times she thought she could have one thing or the other, but she would like to have it all. She wasn't sure if Conner fit that pattern or if he was going to be the reason why she ended up with nothing.

Nichole prepared for her interview with Conner as if she was preparing to interview the President of the United States. She knew she had to have all her questions and follow-ups ready and she knew she had to be on her guard; otherwise Conner would find it easy to distract her.

Her plan—albeit a rough one—was to be professional and not speak about what had happened the night before. But she was tired, and no matter how many cups of coffee she downed, she didn't feel like herself.

The conversation with Willow still weighed on her mind as she got out of a cab in front of the Matchmakers, Inc. offices. She wondered what Gail had felt when she'd first arrived there. She remembered that her friend had decided to go to the matchmaker because she was tired of being alone.

Was that it? Was she tired of being alone too? Was that the reason she was feeling things for Conner she didn't want to? She hoped not. Falling in love didn't figure into her plans until she was closer to forty, and since she was just thirty she had ten years before that happened.

She noticed that most of the professionals she knew lost their edge when they got into their forties. Knowing that, she'd always figured that would be the time she'd settle down. But Conner had shown up now. And he was tempting her in ways she wasn't ready to be tempted.

"Hello, ma'am. Do you have an appointment with one of

the matchmakers today?" the receptionist said as Nichole entered the building.

"No, I don't," Nichole said, pushing her sunglasses up on top of her head. "I'm Nichole Reynolds, here to meet with Conner Macafee."

"Yes, ma'am. He's not here yet, but he said to show you to the conference room."

"Thank you," Nichole said, following the girl down a hallway lined with photos of romantic dates and couples in silhouette.

The conference room had a big picture of a romantic island beach with a couple shown walking away from the camera holding hands. And written on the far end of the wall, in a pretty, scrolling font, were the words *Everyone Deserves to Be Happy Ever After.*

This entire room was designed to make you think of hearts and flowers. Of love and romance and all the dreams that people had when they thought of meeting their soul mate. This room was part of the propaganda of the matchmaking business.

"Would you like something to drink?" the receptionist asked.

"Water would be great," Nichole said. She had dry mouth from all that caffeine she'd ingested today.

The receptionist got her a bottle of water from the refrigerator hidden under the credenza and then left her alone in the room. Nichole used the camera on her phone to take a picture of the room and then jotted down a few notes before the door behind her opened.

She knew without glancing up that it was Conner. It was as if her body had some sort of GPS that notified her when he was in the vicinity.

"Hello, Nichole," he said.

"Hello, Conner. How's your day been so far?" she asked.

"Well, it didn't start off that great since my mistress was missing from my house this morning," he said.

"I had another early meeting," she said.

He stared at her with those shrewd blue eyes of his and she felt as if he could see straight through her. She blinked and glanced down at her notes. "If you'd have a seat, we can get started."

"I don't want to get started yet. Why did you leave this morning without saying goodbye?" he asked.

She chewed her lower lip. She had to play this the right way or she was going to end up saying the wrong thing. But she didn't know how to do that. "I said I had an early meeting. Can we leave it at that? I'll be more than happy to discuss this with you when we are both at your home tonight."

"Very well," he said. He sat down next to her at the conference table instead of across from her. "What do you want to know?"

"Do you mind if I record our interview?" she asked. "That way if I have a question from my notes I can go back and listen to the tape."

"That would be fine," he said.

She took out her iPhone and chose the voice memo app. She set it up between them on the table and hit Record.

"This is my interview with Conner Macafee, owner of Matchmakers, Inc., in their Manhattan offices.

"First of all, how involved are you in the running of the day-to-day operations?" she asked.

"I'm not really involved except from a financial oversight standpoint."

"Why do you own a matchmaking company when marriage is clearly not something you're interested in?" she asked.

He leaned back in his chair and she lifted her phone and

pointed it toward him. "I inherited the company from my maternal grandmother. My original intent was to sell, but I had a friend who was the victim of a gold digger. He ended up with a broken heart so I thought if I kept the company, I could send my friends who were marriage-minded here. Matchmakers, Inc. vets all applicants to prevent the sort of thing that happened to my friend."

"Interesting. So, in a way, in the beginning you were part of the company?" she asked.

"Only as far as my one friend was involved. The matchmakers were already employed and had strong reputations for being good at what they do. I simply added a new step in one of the background checks they were already running."

"The sign on the wall says everyone deserves to be happy ever after. Is that something you want for yourself?" she asked. She knew that this question wasn't just for her interview. Willow had said happy and successful weren't mutually exclusive and Nichole needed to hear Conner's answer so that maybe she could keep herself from falling in love with him.

"I do want that for myself," he said. "I'm just not entirely sure what I need to be happy in a relationship."

The words were unexpected and Nichole glanced up at him to see how intently he was staring at her. He reached over and took her iPhone from her hand and turned off the recording option.

Conner had a sinking feeling that he was losing control of the entire situation with Nichole. Last night he'd had to carry her back to her room because he'd wanted her to sleep in his arms all night and after the night before when that had happened, he knew if he was going to maintain any control over his emotions and keep from letting this mistress thing become a real relationship, he couldn't sleep with her.

Sex was fine, but sleeping with her made him feel things that he couldn't attribute to chemistry. And he knew that was a mistake. From the beginning, Nichole hadn't been like other women and instead of seeing that as a challenge, his mind was saying he should have viewed it as warning.

But he hadn't. And part of him felt as if it was almost too late now. "I want to be happy as much as the next guy."

"I guess that's off the record?" she asked.

"Yes. This is between you and me," he said. "I know you're upset about last night."

She exhaled heavily and put her pen down on the desk. "You are so right I am. But I can't get into that right now. We only have thirty minutes for this interview."

"There's really not much else to say about the company. But I will answer your questions later if they keep coming up."

"Thank you," she said. "So what do you want to discuss?"

He didn't know. Now that he'd pushed to make it personal, he was unsure. Ah, hell, this was a mistake. A big one. He should pretend he'd received a page from the office and leave now.

"I can't sleep with you at night and still be objective about our relationship the next day," he said.

She nibbled on her lower lip and he couldn't resist leaning in to kiss her. She didn't relax into his embrace as she normally did and that was an indication of how upset she still was at him.

"I can't, either. I'm struggling here because I can't tell if what I want is driven by you or by me. I have always had light, no-strings-attached relationships, but with you that doesn't seem to be enough."

He didn't like hearing about her past relationships, even though he knew that was a hypocritical attitude to have. He'd had the same kind of relationships, but he didn't like the thought of any other man touching Nichole intimately. Or knowing her the way he was getting to know her.

"I don't know, either. You are the worst possible woman for me to be in this situation with. You're a reporter—"

"I know. And you are a commitmentphobe," she said. "We aren't exactly each other's perfect mate, but this bargain we struck…it's more complicated than I thought it would be."

He had to admit it was for him, too. He thought they'd have sex, he'd keep her off balance and in a daze, she wouldn't ask too many questions and the month would speed by. Damn, had he been wrong. His objectivity had been compromised as far as she was concerned.

"I'm sorry," he said.

"The worst part is that even after everything that's gone on between us, I'm not sorry."

Those words gave him back the upper hand. He had the feeling that if he was careful in how he handled her from now on, she might be willing to forgive him his shortcomings. And this bargain could still work out for him the way he needed it to.

"We will just have to figure it out as we go along," he said, hoping those words would be enough to keep her happy with him.

"Yes, we will," she said.

"I did have one more question for you," she said.

"Yes?"

"Is there a part of you that wonders whether your parents' relationship would have turned out differently if they had used a service like this one?" she asked.

Just like that, she had the upper hand again. Yes, it was

something he'd debated a million times. When his friend, Grant, had been the victim of a gold digger and Conner had referred him to the matchmaking service, he'd thought of his mom. Would a matchmaker have been able to foresee that his father could create two separate families and never let those lives touch?

He had no idea if that would have mitigated the situation they'd all found themselves in.

"I don't dwell on the past," he said.

"Conner, I gave you access to me in a way I've not given any other man. I expect you to honor our bargain in the same way and answer my questions."

He shoved his chair back from the table and paced away from her. "I can't do that. We didn't agree to how I'd answer your questions. Only that I would."

She stood up as well. "I'm not going to let you push my questions aside. This isn't too personal. It is a simple question."

"It's not simple, as you well know. It's damn complicated and plays on a boy's emotional reactions to a horrible situation with his parents. I'm a man and I run this company for a profit. Sure, it'd be nice to say that I have some kind of romantic delusion about how my parents' marriage could have been saved, but it's simply not true.

"My dad was a duplicitous man—both in how he treated his family and in his shady business dealings. Do I think a matchmaker could have somehow gleaned that about him in a fifteen-minute interview? Doubtful."

Conner knew he needed to stop talking, but the anger he felt at his father was welling up inside him and the anger he felt toward Nichole for making him think about these things and feel the way he used to was huge. He shoved his hands in his pockets and then started walking toward the door of the conference room.

"That last part was off the record—don't print it," he said. "This interview is over for today. I have a dinner meeting tonight and my colleague is bringing his wife. I expect you to attend. My assistant will text you the address and time."

He walked out the door without a backward glance and kept on walking until he was on the street. He ignored the Rolls Royce Phantom parked at the curb and just tried to lose himself in the crowd. He'd like to pretend that the only emotions roiling through him right now were anger, but he also knew there was a bit of sadness tinged with regret when it came to how he'd handled Nichole once again.

Thirteen

Nichole dressed for her dinner with Conner with the most care she'd spent on herself in years. The way he'd left her at Matchmakers, Inc. had shaken her. She intended to follow up with him tonight when they were alone.

But she wanted him off guard. She needed him to be awed by how she looked and to want her to stay in his life.

She was scared because everything he'd said to her made her fall a little more for him. He was wounded and, she had to assume a little threatened by having her in his life. And even though she'd always thought she wasn't one of those women who wanted to heal a man, she did want to help him put his past to rest if she could. She needed to figure out how to fix that for him.

And though she knew there wasn't an easy way to do that, she was tempted to try.

She arrived at Del Posto, the restaurant in the Meatpacking District owned by celebrity chef Mario Batali.

Nichole had never eaten there before. Conner was waiting in the crowded lobby for her.

He smiled when she walked over to him, making her realize he was going to pretend that nothing had happened earlier between them. She leaned up and kissed his cheek.

"Thanks for getting here on time. Cam and Becca Stern aren't going to be meeting us for another ten minutes," Conner said. "I wanted a chance to give you some background on them before they arrived."

"Shoot," she said. "If you'd texted me the names earlier I would have done a Google search on them."

"Good idea. If we do this again I'll definitely do that. Cam is the co-owner of Luna Azul in Miami. It's one of the hottest nightclubs on the East Coast."

"I'm familiar with it. Nate Stern, his younger brother, is my contact in Miami and South Beach for gossip. He used to be a baseball player."

"Good. So you're familiar with them. I'm one of the investors in a second location for Luna Azul here in Manhattan and tonight's dinner is to discuss some of the details of that. But since he's brought his wife, I think it will be more social," Conner said, leading her into the bar area. "Everything said businesswise would have to be off the record."

"I know that," she said. "But thank you for always being so official."

"That was sarcasm, right?" he asked.

"Yup. When are you going to realize—never mind. You're never going to see me as a different type of reporter from the guy who duped you when you were young."

He shook his head. "I'm trying. What can I get you to drink?"

"A bellini," she said. The sweet peach and prosecco drink was exactly what she needed to relax and just let the evening progress. She was beginning to suspect that being a mistress meant pushing emotions to the very bottom. How else did women survive in this position?

She knew she should be thinking of their arrangement as a business deal—exactly what Conner had told her to do in the beginning, but she hadn't been able to. She didn't want to. It was too intimate for that and every time they were together—not just sexually—it was harder for her to keep the line between personal and professional clear.

Conner came back with the drinks. He handed her glass to her and then lifted his own. "A toast."

"To?"

"To you, Nichole, for putting up with me and making me want to be a better man," he said.

Damn, why had he said that? She clinked her glass to his and started to say something when a couple joined them. She took a sip of her drink while Conner shook hands with Cam Stern. They were the same height. Cam was tan, as befitted a man who lived in Miami. He kept one arm wrapped around his wife's waist and she smiled up at him.

"Introduce us to your lady," Cam said.

"Becca and Cam Stern, this is Nichole Reynolds," Conner said.

Nichole held her hand out to each of them and they both shook it.

"I know your name," Becca said. "I read your column online every day."

"Thanks," Nichole said. "I also talk to your brother-in-law frequently to keep up-to-date on what's going on in your neck of the woods."

"I'm confused," Cam said. "Conner, did you know you were dating a reporter?"

"Of course I did, Cam," Conner said.

Cam winked at Nichole. "Sorry, my dear, but he's always said reporters were the scourge of the earth."

"I'm trying to bring him around to a new way of thinking," she said.

"Is it working?" Cam asked.

Conner snaked his arm around her waist and pulled her close for a quick kiss. "She's got her ways of making me forget she's a reporter."

Nichole knew that wasn't true, but quickly picked up on the fact that, for tonight at least, he wanted Cam and Becca to see them as a couple. Not a man and his mistress.

Luckily, the hostess called them and they were seated in a private area. Dinner was a lively affair that mainly consisted of general conversation. As Conner had suspected, the inclusion of the women made it a social evening instead of a strictly business meeting.

Nichole learned that Becca and Cam had a son who'd recently turned two. Becca was a doting mom who thought her son was a genius. Cam was proud of his boy as well and both parents had more than one time during the evening pulled out their cell phone to show off pictures of their child.

"Are you planning for more children?" Nichole asked.

"Yes, as a matter of fact, Becca just learned she's three months' pregnant," Cam said.

"Congratulations," Conner said.

"You thinking about starting a family soon?" Cam said to Conner. "Now that you've found a woman like Nichole."

Nichole looked over at Conner and wondered what he'd say to that. She didn't feel that either of them was ready for a family at this point.

"We're still getting to know each other and enjoying our relationship. We aren't that serious," Conner said and turned the conversation away from them.

Nichole knew that he could have said she's my mistress and we just have sex, so she counted herself lucky that he hadn't. It was the kind of comment she'd made a million times in the past about someone she was dating and she knew the words shouldn't have hurt her, but deep inside they did.

Nichole had been avoiding him for the last five days. When they'd come home from dinner with Cam and Becca, she'd said she had menstrual cramps and rushed off to her bed alone. The next day she'd been gone before he got up again.

He knew something was the matter because she'd even turned down his invitation to the party at his mother's house—he had thought she wanted to observe him with his family. He'd gone against his better judgment in inviting her, hoping she'd see it as the olive branch he'd meant it to be. But she'd declined.

That night, he sent Randall to pick her up after work and bring her back to his apartment. He'd had to cancel all his plans for the evening, but he didn't care what happened. He was going to get to the bottom of whatever was going on between them. If she wanted to back out, well, then, he'd have to think it over.

She had enough to run a story about his involvement with Matchmakers, Inc. and the television show. But she'd always wanted more from him. He'd tried to deliver it, but in the end he didn't know if he'd ever be able to give her what she really wanted.

She walked in the front door of the apartment around 7:30 and put her keys on the table near the door.

"I can't believe you had Randall practically kidnap me," she said, hands on her hips. She wore a pencil skirt with a button-down blouse tucked into it. Her hair was in a high ponytail and she had a pair of designer shades pushed up on her head.

"I asked you to dinner," he said.

"And I said not tonight," she said.

"Well, our agreement was for every night," he said. "And you've been avoiding me. We need to talk. Since you've been doing your level best to avoid me, I had no other choice. Come in and sit down. I've poured you a glass of wine," he said.

She walked across the floor with that slow gliding gait of hers and he watched her move. God, he wanted this woman. The two nights she'd spent in his arms hadn't been nearly enough.

Part of him suspected a million nights wouldn't be enough but he wasn't going to have that many, so he'd have to make do with this time they had together.

She sat down on the edge of the couch and took the wineglass he held out to her. Conner was nervous, and that annoyed him. In fact he hadn't been this nervous since the first time he'd walked into the board of directors meeting for Macafee International and told them that he was ready to run the company.

He took a swallow of the scotch and soda he'd poured for himself and then sat down next to her on the couch.

"Why are you hiding from me?" he asked, point blank. "I'd come to expect you to be someone who would confront a problem, not avoid it."

She took a sip of her wine and then set the glass on the coffee table. "I am normally a person who faces things head-on, but I didn't know how to handle this. We have an agreement, we aren't in a normal relationship, as you sort of stated to your friends at dinner the other night."

He shoved his hand through his hair, something he

knew was a bad habit. "I didn't say anything about us that wasn't true."

She frowned a little. "I know. I guess I had started thinking that we might have something more between us."

"Like what?"

She took another sip of her wine and then put the glass down. "Despite the agreement, I'm starting to care for you, Conner."

"I care for you, too."

She smiled at him then. She took her sunglasses from her head and tossed them on the table. "I hoped you would. I didn't know how else to deal with this. I've never been in a relationship where I was so concerned about making it work, but I am with you."

"That's flattering and I'd love to see this work out for us, too, but I'm not sure…"

He stood up and walked to the windows to look down at the city. He knew something about himself that he'd never shared with anyone else. He was very afraid that he was like his father in more than just business. He might be the kind of man who was incapable of loving anyone.

He cared deeply for his sister and his mother, but that didn't feel like love. And though he had to be honest and say that Nichole mattered more to him than he'd ever thought any woman could, he didn't see it developing any further.

He wanted her. He lusted after her as if he'd never been with a woman before and had just discovered sex. But it was more than that.

"What aren't you sure about?" she asked him.

"I'm not sure I have any more to offer you than what we have right now," he said.

"I don't know that I do, either. Why don't we both try it together?"

He was tempted by what she was offering, but he knew he'd be lying to her if he let her in any further. "Red, I would love to say yes and become that happily-ever-after guy you asked me about at the Matchmakers, Inc. office, but I'm not that kind of guy."

"You're just afraid to take a chance," she said. "You can love. I'm scared, too."

He wasn't afraid of her or of caring for her. "I'm not afraid."

"Yes, you are. Whatever is going on inside you is fear. I know you can love. I've seen you with your mom and your sister," she said.

"You're grasping at straws," he said, shutting down all his emotions instead of letting her get through to him. He wasn't going to give that kind of power over himself to anyone, especially Nichole.

"I can't," he said. "I like you, you're sexy and you amuse me, but that's all this can ever be. I don't feel that deep bond with you that could be love."

"I don't believe you."

"Then you're fooling yourself. Love is a superficial emotion that people use to make excuses for their own lack of control. I'm not one of those people."

Nichole saw how sincere Conner was as he confessed that he couldn't love her because love was superficial. But she didn't believe it. She could see fear in him because it was the same thing she had inside of her.

She didn't know what the future held. She'd seen her parents stick together to their own detriment early in their marriage, but then they had figured out a way to make it work. And her father had always said it was the love he felt for her mom that had helped them survive as a couple.

"Love isn't superficial," she said. "I don't think you believe that, either. That's the reason why you didn't throw me out of your office that first day. And it's also why you invited me to go to your mom's party this weekend. You do care about me, Conner. And there isn't anything you can say that will change my mind. Why not give us a chance?"

She could see the conflict within him as he watched her. There was a longing in his eyes that made her want to say just forget it, but she knew she couldn't keep on this way. From the beginning, the illicit thrill of thinking of herself as Conner's mistress had been exciting, but the reality had always made her hurt deep inside.

She wasn't sure if it was just that she had recognized him as…her soul mate. They were so similar in many things, especially in how both of them were afraid to let anyone too close. Yet Nichole was willing to take a chance. Willing to give Conner entrée into her life and into her heart. Clearly, he wasn't willing to do the same.

"I can't," he said at last. "When my dad left, the way he left, I decided that no one would have that kind of power over my life. No one would hurt me that way again or disappoint me the way he did."

"I won't—"

"You have no idea if you will or not. The thing I learned from that is that I have to control who I let into my life. And what I've found to be true is that I function better when I'm not involved with anyone.

"I thought that by making you my mistress, by keeping in mind that you were a reporter, I'd be able to keep you in one neat, safe corner of my life. We would make love and enjoy superficial conversations, but that's it. That's where it would all end."

"But it didn't work out that way, did it?" she asked. His words were like a dagger in her heart. He was telling her he was too afraid to take a chance on love. And Nichole had just realized with Conner that she was the kind of woman who needed to take a chance on love to really experience it.

It was only standing here with him that made her see that all the light, fun relationships she'd had were meant to safeguard her heart. By keeping it light, she'd stayed safe until she met the one man she didn't want to keep out.

And he was afraid to take a gamble on her...on them.

"We already have found more than that. Well, I have," she said. "I think that you have, too. Otherwise, you wouldn't be so worried about letting me sleep in the same bed as you."

He thrust his hands through his hair until it was disheveled. He was agitated and she could tell that she was making her point with him. She felt a little ray of hope deep inside that she might be able to get through to him. Might be able to convince him that a real relationship was what they both needed.

"Don't read too much into that," he said carefully. "You are my mistress and it is important that you have your own living space."

"Too late. I already have," she said. She realized that she was seeing Conner the way she wanted him to be and not at all sure she was seeing him as he really was. "Tell me that you care about me."

"Why?"

"I need something to hang my hope on. I will stay with you and wait for you to get comfortable with having me in your life, but I need to know that you are capable of feeling something for me."

He paced around the room behind the couch and she watched him walking back and forth. It seemed to her that he was weighing his decision very carefully. She could see the tension inside him and had never seen him like this before.

"Conner."

"Yes?" he asked, looking at her.

She had the feeling she might have asked him for too much. Might have pushed him too far in her bid to get to the heart of what he really felt for her. But she also knew she had no choice. She couldn't keep living with him and pretending that it was okay that she was his mistress.

She wanted to feel safe enough to fall in love with him. Hell, who was she kidding? She was already in love with him, and now feeling so vulnerable she was looking for him to let her know she hadn't fallen alone.

She walked around to him and wrapped her arms around him. She hugged him close, trying to let her feelings surround him. "I'm not sure of this, either, but I'm willing to take a chance."

He hugged her close and she felt the terrible fist in her stomach start to loosen. He lowered his head and breathed in the scent of her hair and then he tipped her head up and she met that blue gaze of his, but she couldn't read any emotion in his eyes.

His mouth descended to hers and his tongue swept over her lips into her mouth. The kiss was long and sweet and as he pulled back from her she realized it was goodbye.

"I can't give you more than this," he said, tracing the line of her cheekbone with his forefinger.

She felt a stab of disappointment and, if she was honest, pain that he'd rejected her love. "I can't do this any longer. I'm going to leave."

"Don't do that."

"I have to," she said.

"What about your story?" he asked.

She felt how desperate he must be to keep her here to use that as a reason for her to stay. And that made the hurt in her heart that much keener. "I have everything I need to write my story."

She picked up her purse and walked slowly to her bedroom where she packed up her overnight bag and got her laptop. Conner didn't follow her and when she came back into the living room he stood in the exact same place.

She walked as slowly as she could to the door, hoping he'd call out that he'd changed his mind and stop her from leaving, but he didn't.

She got to the elevator and realized that she was crying and felt stupid that she was. She hadn't cried like this since the day she'd found her mother lying on the floor next to her bed. She hadn't hurt like this since then, either. And part of her wondered if Conner even knew what he was doing. Was life safer when you kept everyone out?

Fourteen

The next week was the longest of Conner's life. He focused on business, staying long hours at the office because when he went home it felt empty. Even though Nichole hadn't been in his home for that long, she'd left her trace in every room of the apartment.

He'd dealt with this kind of feeling before, but it had been a long time ago. He knew he'd made a mistake when he'd let her go, but given the way he felt now he also knew that it had been the right decision. As hard as it was, he was dealing with her absence in his life and he would just soldier on.

He'd had Mrs. Plumb pack the remainder of her belongings and then Randall had taken them back to her house. There was no sign of her left anywhere in the apartment, but he still felt her there. He spent too much time late at night standing in the doorway of the guest bedroom and wondering how much his carrying her back to her bed had contributed to her leaving.

His iPhone rang and he glanced at the screen to see it was his sister. He didn't want to talk to her so he ignored the call. He left his office and headed downstairs to the gym in his building. Maybe running would take his mind off Nichole.

He'd been reading her column every day, telling himself it was to see if she'd written her article on him yet, but he hadn't seen it. And part of him hoped it took her a while to write it because as long as she didn't he'd have the excuse to go and look at her picture.

She was a good writer, something he'd known since they'd first met, and he was surprised at how much she made him laugh when he read about the different people she reported on. Part of it was the way she captured the people that he knew pretty well; the other part was her wry take on life.

The current couple being taped for *Sexy & Single* were finally falling for each other and reading her columns about their love was just a tad painful. He knew that it was his own perception coloring what he read, but also felt that she was directing some jabs at him.

This morning's column, in particular, had hit a nerve, when she wrote about how Paul wasn't afraid to take a chance on letting Rikki into his life.

Those were practically the same words she'd said to him when she left. He still remembered how slowly she'd walked to the door. He wished he'd stopped her.

He got changed in the locker room and then walked into the main gym. His phone beeped, sending him an alert that he had mentions on Twitter. His sister was tweeting about him again.

But he didn't call her. He wasn't ready to talk to Jane

or his mom. He'd been avoiding both of them for the last week because he didn't want to deal with their questions about Nichole and he knew they'd have them.

He switched his iPhone to airplane mode, put on his exercise playlist, which featured lots of heavy metal from the '80s, and started running.

As AC/DC's *Back in Black* blared in his ears, he tried to put some distance between himself and his feelings for Nichole. But her face was there in his mind as he ran. The harder he pushed himself, the more he saw her. That impish, sexy grin on the Fourth of July. How earthy and sensual she'd looked that first night in his apartment in those damn skintight jeans and that tank top. The way she'd looked when she'd told him the terrible secret of her past. That vulnerability that she hadn't hidden from him, even though she didn't have to share what she was feeling with him.

Thirty minutes later he slowed his pace to a cool-down run, no closer to getting Nichole out of his mind than he'd been when he started. He got off the treadmill, switched his phone back on and found he'd missed three calls from Jane. He was planning to continue ignoring her until he got her text.

I'm worried about you. Call me.

He didn't want her worrying about him. He showered and then called her back.

"It's about time," Jane said. "Where the hell have you been?"

"Working, Janey."

"Mom is driving in from the Hamptons because she hasn't spoken to you in over a week."

"She doesn't need to do that," Conner said. "Let me call her and talk to her."

"Too late. We're descending on you. What's up?" she asked. "You haven't been like this…I can't remember the last time you completely shut down this way. And don't say it's business because I know you don't have any big deals going on right now."

"What do you mean descending on me?"

"We're coming to your place," she said.

"I'll come to you," he said. He didn't want to go to his apartment right now himself, nor have either of them there for that matter. "I'm on my way as we speak."

"Conner, are you okay?" she asked.

"Yes. I've just been really busy at work," he said.

"Okay. Are you bringing Nichole with you?" she asked. "I liked her and Mom wants to meet her."

Of course his mom wanted to meet her. Thanks to Jane's blabbing, she thought that Nichole and he were a couple. And thanks to his own blundering, that wasn't true anymore. "No, I'm not. We're no longer dating."

"Oh," Jane said. "Why not?"

"She wanted something from me I couldn't give her," Conner said after a long pause.

"What did she want?" Jane asked.

"Probably the same thing that Palmer wants from you," Conner said.

"What's wrong with us?" Jane asked. "Why can't we fall in love?"

"I don't know, Janey. I guess we're both afraid of the consequences."

"I think you're right," she said. "I wish we weren't."

"Well, it's not too late for you to change. Palmer isn't like Dad."

"You know the scary part is that I get that. But I'm still afraid to trust him."

Conner knew exactly what his sister was feeling in that regard. "I know."

Conner didn't want to think about how different Nichole was or how much he cared about her. He just wanted to find a numb place in his emotions and figure out how to keep living without her. The price of having her back in his life was too high, and one he wasn't willing to pay.

The first week after leaving Conner had been the hardest. She spent a lot of time at work writing about the lives of others. The hardest thing to write about was the progress of Paul and Rikki on the set of *Sexy & Single*.

It was amazing for her to see how much Rikki had changed over the course of their dates. They were at the halfway point in their televised dates and Nichole could see the couple falling in love. And seeing what a healthy relationship looked like made her wish that Conner could be a different kind of man. But in her heart she knew she wouldn't have fallen for him if he'd been anyone other than himself.

. She'd found herself subsisting on coffee mostly. The second week after she left him, she woke on a Sunday morning and decided she didn't want to leave her apartment.

She moved her Keurig machine into the living room, put *Romancing the Stone* into her DVD player and sat there crying, wishing that Conner would unexpectedly show up on her doorstep and tell her that he loved her.

A knock on her door startled her because she rarely… okay, *never* had guests. She couldn't help the hope that blossomed in her heart as she walked to the door. She knew she looked terrible with her hair unbrushed and still in her PJs at three in the afternoon, but she didn't care.

She looked through the peephole and saw Gail and Willow standing there. She patted down her hair, undid the security locks and opened the door.

"I told you she must be sick," Gail said, coming into the apartment and looking around the room.

"She's not sick," Willow said. "She's hiding."

"Why are you two here?" Nichole asked.

"You missed brunch," Willow said. "You never miss brunch unless you text us and you didn't. Are you okay?"

She had forgotten it was the fourth Sunday of the month. "Oh, God, I'm sorry. I just lost track of the days."

Gail put her hand on Nichole's forehead. "You don't have a fever, but your eyes are watery and your nose is red."

Willow was walking around her small living room and saw the coffee machine on the end table and the pile of tissues on the couch. "Why is the Keurig in the living room?"

"I didn't want to have to walk to the kitchen," Nichole said.

"Is this about Conner?" Willow asked.

Nichole thought about lying to her friends, telling them that she had been working hard and needed a pajama day, but they'd both listened to her to as she'd tried to figure out what to do with him so they'd know she was lying. "It's over with him and me."

"Why didn't you call us?" Gail asked. "I know how hard it was for you to decide to live with him."

Nichole went over to the couch and sat down. Gail and Willow did the same. "I didn't want to talk about him. I'm still trying to figure out how I feel about everything."

"Tell us what happened," Will said.

"I fell in love with him. I should have known when my

instincts were telling me not to agree to be his mistress that it was because I cared about him.

"He isn't the type of man who feels safe being in love. He's afraid, I think. Oh, I really don't know what he thinks, but I asked him to give us a chance and he said no."

"Why?"

"He doesn't believe in love," Nichole said. "I get why. I mean his father did a number on him when he left in the middle of a scandal. And Conner never had a chance to talk to him because of that plane crash that killed him."

"He has issues," Gail said. "Can you get him to talk to you about it?"

"No. He doesn't want to. He likes the way his life is. He likes being alone. I thought I did, too, until I met him."

"I'm sorry," Gail said.

"Me, too. Do we hate him?" Willow asked.

"No, we don't hate him. I feel sorry for him. And I'm trying very hard to fall out of love with him," Nichole said.

"Is it working?" Willow asked.

"Not so far…I was hoping you guys would be him."

"I'm sorry we weren't," Gail said. "You need to get out of this apartment if you're going to forget him."

"I do?"

"Yes, as long as you stay home all you'll do is think about him. Russell and I are going sailing this afternoon. Why don't you come with us?"

Nichole loved her friend dearly, but the last thing she wanted to do was spend the afternoon with a couple who were clearly in love. Especially not sailing, when she remembered that it was Conner's favorite hobby.

"No, thanks," Nichole said. "I'm watching *Jewel of the Nile* next."

"No, you can't watch romantic movies now. It will just keep feeding your hopes," Willow said.

"I know, but I want to. I need to do this," Nichole said. "I'm going to be fine. It's just a broken heart. Hopefully, over time, it will heal."

"Do you want to be alone?" Gail asked.

"Today, yes, but not forever. I think I'm mourning what might have been and the sad part is I know that it's just my dreams of what might have been. Conner never did or said anything to make me believe he'd be different."

"None of that matters, does it?" Willow asked.

"Nope," Nichole said. "Have fun sailing this afternoon, Gail."

"Are you sure you'll be okay?" she asked.

"Yes, I'm fine. You both can go," Nichole said.

"I'll stay," Willow volunteered.

"You hate *Jewel of the Nile* and I don't want to hear your snide comments about the plotting," Nichole said.

Willow laughed and Nichole felt a little better knowing that she had these women as her friends. "I just need to feel sorry for myself for today. I'll snap out of it soon and be back to my old self."

Her friends left and slowly she found that she did start to feel better. She still missed Conner, but the reality of knowing he was truly out of her life forced her to start adjusting to living without him. She'd write her story about him and then hopefully be able to move on.

Summer had finally waned and it was fall. Conner would like to say that with the passing of time he'd stopped thinking about Nichole all the time, but he hadn't.

He was alternately annoyed at himself and angry with her for making him still feel something after all this time. She'd written her column about Matchmakers, Inc. and he'd enjoyed reading it, but she'd never written the story about him and the past. The one that he'd feared she'd write. He saw that as proof that she had more integrity than he'd thought she did.

He wished that he could find a way to meet her again and start over, but he knew that he'd never do it. He hated that even though it had been two months since she'd walked out his door, a day hadn't gone by when he didn't think of her.

He'd been invited to the finale of the third couple's matchmaking episodes on *Sexy & Single* and he was attending. He told himself and his assistant that he was going because it was expected of him. But the truth was he knew that Willow was a good friend of Nichole's and he hoped that either Nichole would be there or he'd be able to bring her name up to Willow and find out how she was.

The finale was being held as the first one had been, in a large ballroom in the Big Apple Kiwi Klub. Russell Holloway had allowed the *Sexy & Single* TV show to shoot there in exchange for some free publicity. Conner couldn't help but remember the lunch he'd had at the Klub with Nichole. It was on that day that she'd agreed to be his.

A big part of him wished he'd taken better care of how he'd kept her. He wondered if she'd still be in his bed—no she wouldn't, he thought. He'd only asked for her to be his mistress for a month.

He knew now that a month wouldn't have been long enough. He was starting to think a lifetime wouldn't be long enough, but he knew that wasn't in the cards. Hell, he didn't want it to be. He didn't want her back because she made him vulnerable and yet all he thought about when he wasn't working was how to get her back.

He walked into the ballroom and saw his friend, Russell, standing off to one side. Russell waved Conner over and he walked across the ballroom, scanning the crowd for Nichole. He didn't see his sexy redhead.

But she wasn't his. He'd kicked her out of his life—rather, let her walk out of his life—and he had to move on. He was starting to feel as if he was obsessed with her.

"Hey, Conner, how's things?" Russell said as he joined the other man.

"Can't complain," Conner said.

"I haven't seen you at the yacht club lately," Russell remarked.

"I've been busy with work," Conner said. And he had been. His staff were all complaining about the hours he'd been putting in because he'd been demanding they work just as hard as he did. He knew he'd become a tyrant at work, but it was the only time he stopped thinking about Nichole, so he had to stay there longer.

"I know how that is. I'm leaving next week to break ground on my first family-destination resort."

"How's that going?" Conner asked.

"Good. It's a totally different market and I love the challenge of figuring it out," Russell said.

"Is Gail going with you to the groundbreaking?" Conner asked. He remembered that Gail was one of Nichole's good friends, too.

"She is. I told her I needed my fiancée by my side," Russell said.

"Yes, he did," Gail said, joining the men. "And since the first resort is in L.A., I thought I could combine it with a work trip. I have some clients I'm going to meet with out there."

Conner wanted to play it cool and try to ask some innocuous question about Nichole, but he couldn't. "Hi, Gail, how is Nichole?" he blurted out.

"She's good. But you should ask her yourself," Gail said. "She's over there."

Conner turned his head to see that Nichole had entered

the ballroom while he'd been talking to Russell. She looked good. She was thinner than he remembered, her cheek-bones more pronounced. Her hair seemed thicker than he remembered, too. He stood there staring at her, his eyes slowly skimming over her body until his gaze dropped to her stomach and he noticed a small bump.

He started walking toward her, wondering if he was seeing things. But he knew her body intimately and she hadn't been like this before. She glanced up as she saw him walking toward her and broke off her conversation.

"Can I have a word with you in private?" Conner asked.

She nodded and pivoted on her heel, walking out of the ballroom and down the hall where there was a bench tucked into a small alcove.

He followed her, thinking how much he'd missed seeing her. His mind was also going over the possibility that she might be pregnant. He remembered that the second time they'd made love, he hadn't used protection.

"What can I do for you?" she asked, stopping at the bench.

"Are you pregnant?" he asked.

"Yes."

"Why didn't you call and tell me?" he demanded. He couldn't process everything at once and clung to some anger to see him through this encounter. He was con-flicted. He wanted to pull her into his arms and kiss her, but he also wanted to know why she hadn't let him know about the baby because that would have been enough of a reason for him to demand she come back into his life.

"Why would I?" she asked.

"I am the father of your child," he said. He didn't ask, because he knew Nichole well enough to know she'd never move on to another man that quickly, despite the serial dating he knew she'd done before him. He'd been as different for her as she'd been for him. And she'd said she loved him.

He hadn't forgotten that. Hell. Dammit to hell. He suddenly realized that the reason he hadn't been able to forget about her was that he loved her. But now it didn't matter. She'd think he was telling her what she wanted to hear for the baby's sake.

It was too late.

Fifteen

Nichole didn't know what to say to Conner. How could she put into words that she wanted him to come back to her for her—not for a baby? She just hadn't figured that out, and no matter how many late-night gab-fests she'd had with her girlfriends, she hadn't come up with a solution.

"I didn't think you'd care," she said at last. She should have been better prepared to see him, but she hadn't been. She noticed that he'd had his hair cut and she longed to run her fingers through his hair. He was cleanly shaved, but looked tired.

She'd missed him. Couldn't help but sleep hugging the pillow he'd slept on that one night he'd spent in her bed. She often thought of what she'd say to her child when that child asked about his father, but she didn't have words for that yet, either.

"Why wouldn't I care?" he asked.

"You said that you didn't need me in your life. I'm pretty

sure when I walked out the door you planned to never see me again. Why would a child make any difference?"

"Because it's my child," he said.

He put his hand out to her, but she stepped back. If he touched her, she was either going to start crying or jump into his arms and neither of those actions was something she wanted to do right now. She needed to keep her cool and let this play out.

"So you want me in your life for the child?" she asked. "That's not acceptable to me."

She could see how conflicted he was and wanted to offer him some kind of emotional help, but she knew herself well enough to realize that she couldn't put him first. From the moment she'd found out she was pregnant, she'd stopped moping around with her broken heart.

She'd never expected a child to give her hope. But that's what her pregnancy had done for her. All the unwanted love she had for Conner she could pour into the child that was growing inside her. And that was what she'd done.

"I'm sorry you feel that way, but I do want my child," he said.

Nichole realized that part of her had been hoping he'd say he wanted her, too, but she knew she had to stop hoping that Conner would react the way she wanted him to. "We can discuss that some other time. I need to get back into the ballroom."

"No," he said. "We need to finish talking about this now. I want you to move back into my apartment so I can take care of you while you're pregnant."

She shook her head. "Why do you need me to do that?" she asked.

"I…for the baby, of course."

"Oh, for the baby," she said. "Then my answer is no.

We can discuss some kind of custody arrangement once the child is born."

She turned to walk away and Conner grabbed her arm and stopped her. "Why won't you at least try to work this out with me?"

"Because I need something from you that you can't give me. You said you couldn't trust someone to be there for you. I don't mean *someone,* I mean me. And when it was just me you couldn't love or care for, then I probably would have gone back to you. You have no idea how much I've missed you," she said. Admitting out loud what she'd felt for him was so cathartic.

"I've missed you, too," he said.

"You have?" she asked.

"Yes."

"Why haven't you called me?" she asked, suspecting that Conner was going to say whatever he had to to get her to do what he wanted. She hated that that was her first reaction, but until he gave her some sign that he really cared for her, she wasn't going to just blindly trust him. She couldn't.

If he broke her heart again, she knew she'd never recover from it.

"I was getting on without you," he said.

"What's changed?" she asked, hoping for just a tiny sign that he loved her.

"Seeing you today. Knowing that you're going to have my baby," he said.

The baby. This was why, despite Gail's urging her to tell Conner, she hadn't. He didn't want her and if she wasn't pregnant, he wouldn't be here trying to talk her into coming back now.

"I'm sorry, Conner, but that's not good enough," she said.

He pushed his hands through his hair the way he did

whenever he was agitated and stared at her. She sensed for a minute that he might understand what she needed from him and she waited, hoping one last time that he'd say what she needed to hear.

"This is all I have," he said at last. "I can't be someone I'm not."

She knew that. She reached up and squeezed his shoulder before pulling her arm out of his grasp. "I know you can't. Please don't blame me for hoping that you could be."

She walked away and this time wasn't any easier than the first time she'd walked away from him. It was what she needed to do, so she kept on walking without looking back at him.

When she entered the ballroom and saw all the trappings of romance, it hit her hard. Why hadn't she fallen in love with a man who could love her back?

What was it about her that led her to men who only wanted fun and no commitment? And why, when her own desires had changed, hadn't fate sent her a man who wanted the same things she wanted?

She realized that she was on the verge of crying and tried to find a quiet place to retreat, but when she turned toward the door she saw Conner standing there. They stared at each other for long minutes and Nichole felt her heart beat so heavy in her chest. Finally, Conner lifted his hand and waved at her before turning and walking away.

And Nichole realized there was something worse than that long lonely walk she'd just taken down the hall away from Conner.

Watching him walk away from her. She knew that no matter what the future held for their child, this was the moment of finality between the two of them and he wasn't ever coming back to her.

* * *

Saturday morning Conner was woken up by a call from his mother. "Good morning, Conner. Have you seen the *America Today Weekend Magazine?*"

Conner sat up in bed and looked at the clock with bleary eyes. After seeing Nichole last night, he'd come home and hit the bottle heavily. It was only 7:00 a.m. His head was pounding and he felt like hell. What had his mom asked?

"What?"

"There is an article about us in *America Today,*" she said. "Have you read it?"

"No. What do you mean us?"

"Our family…well, sort of you. Do you want me to read it to you?"

"Sure," he said. Dammit, he thought…what the hell had she written?

"'Behind the Scenes with the Rich and Famous, by Nichole Reynolds.

"'Like many of you I grew up reading about the wealthy and the powerful. As a teenager, I envied their lives of privilege, their cars and clothes. As I got older and established myself as a writer for *America Today,* I started to gain some more insight into their lives.

"'I saw that behind the privileged facade many of them had worries and concerns that never really touched my life. But it wasn't until I sat down to write an article about Conner Macafee that this was driven home.

"'Like the rest of you, I often wondered what was hiding behind his frosty blue gaze and how the scandal that had surrounded his father and his father's death had affected him. I wanted to know this not because it would bring me anything I could use in my life, but simply because it was a juicy story.

"'I never thought about the impact writing about the rich and famous has on them. Now, some people court publicity, but Conner always shied away from it and that whetted my appetite to know more. When I did finally have a chance to talk to him, I was surprised to find him relatable and human.

"'His family wasn't the dysfunctional mess that many of ours would be if something similar had happened in our lives. His mother, sister and he are very close, with a tight bond of love that flows between them, and they've moved on with their lives the way that true families do by supporting each other.

"'And this reporter has figured out that leaving their past in the past was the best thing that I could do. Examining his life taught me an important lesson in dealing with moving on. I can only hope that I would deal with that kind of incident with as much dignity as the entire Macafee clan has.'

"That's it. What a nice piece," his mom said. "Why did you let her go?"

Conner was still taking in what Nichole had written. It wasn't about them at all, but about him. And he almost felt as if it was written to him. "I was afraid of keeping her in my life."

He heard his mother sigh. "I made a mistake all those years ago, son. When everything happened with your father, I ran away and took you and Janey with me. I stopped going to charity events, I tried to hide, but that wasn't smart of me."

"You did the best you could, Mom," Conner said.

"I put myself first and set a bad example for you and your sister. Instead of staying put and figuring out how to move on, I hid from my own heartbreak and made the two of you afraid to take a chance on love. That was never my intent."

"I don't blame you at all."

"You blame your father," she said. "And I did, too, but the fact is he's gone and we all should leave him in the past, as Nichole said. And I want you to have a shot at a real future."

Conner did, too. "Mom, what if I'm like Dad and one woman isn't enough for me?"

"You have never been serious about any woman and I'm guessing from what Jane said that you are about this one. Just her, am I right?" his mom asked.

"Yes."

"Your father always loved all women. I had to fight for him and it was a constant battle to keep his attention on me. Don't think you are anything like him."

He hadn't remembered that until his mother said it. His father had been a world-class flirt, and there hadn't been a woman in their lives that he hadn't tried to charm. "I guess I don't want to let her in. What if I can't make it work?"

"Being in love is the greatest feeling in the world, and even if it doesn't work out, no one can ever take that from you. But you have to take the chance on it first," she said.

Her words set something free in him. "Thanks, Mom."

"You're welcome, son. Am I going to meet Nichole soon?"

"If I have anything to say about it, you will," Conner said. His head was still pounding, but he didn't feel quite so tired. He hung up with his mom and got out of bed, knowing he had to come up with a plan to get Nichole back.

He showered and shaved and stared at himself in the mirror, but he still had no idea what to do. He only knew that he wanted her back.

Finally he did the only thing he could do. Picking up the phone, he dialed her number and waited.

She didn't answer, so he left her a voice mail. "This is Conner. I read the article in *America Today Weekend Magazine* and we need to talk."

He hung up and waited five minutes before he called back again, but when she didn't answer, he simply hung up. He needed to get other things in place, as well.

He loved her and he wanted to make sure she knew it. He left his apartment and went to the jewelry store to buy her two pieces of jewelry. The first was an engagement ring, because he couldn't tell her he loved her and then not ask her to share the rest of his life with him.

The second was a charm bracelet, which he hadn't intended to buy, but when he saw the Swarovski crystal fireworks charm, he thought of her and the day they'd met. How fireworks had sparked between the two of them. He imagined he would fill the bracelet with other charms as their life together progressed.

He ordered flowers and champagne and then went back home to wait for her call. She finally called him at three in the afternoon, just as he was about to go to her place and find her.

"Hello, Nichole," he said.

"Hi, Conner. What's up?" she asked.

"I need you to come to my place to discuss the article you wrote."

"I don't know if that's a good idea," she said.

"Please," he said. "I think after everything we've been through you could come over here."

She sighed. "Okay, it might take me some time to get a cab."

"Randall is waiting outside your building for you," he said.

He hung up and glanced around the room to make sure everything was just as he wanted. Then he sat down to wait out the longest fifteen minutes of his life. When he heard the elevator bing and then her footsteps on the tile outside the front door, he wiped his sweating palms on his pant legs and hoped that she still loved him enough to take him back.

Nichole couldn't believe she'd returned to Conner's apartment. She wanted to pretend she was doing it for their unborn child, but she knew that part of her still hoped things could work out between them.

He opened the door before she got to it and she stopped in her tracks. Seeing him standing there just reminded her of the painful way they had said goodbye the last time. And she realized that no matter how much she hoped it might be different, this meeting would more than likely end in the same painful way.

Was she some kind of masochist to keep doing this to herself?

"Come in," he said, stepping back.

She started to walk over the threshold, but as she brushed past him, Conner pulled her into his arms. He held her so tightly to him that she felt that glimmer of hope deep inside her again.

He tipped her head up to his and kissed her slowly. His hands slid down her back and he pulled her so close to him that she couldn't help but believe he'd invited her here today because he finally realized he cared about her.

He lifted her into his arms and carried her into his apartment. She saw that roses were covering every surface in the living room as he set her down on the couch. Instead of sitting down beside her, he stood next to her.

"Thank you for coming here today," he said.

"You're welcome. I'm sorry I didn't send you an advance copy of the article."

"That's fine. I didn't call you to talk about that."

"Why did you call me, then?" she asked.

He shoved his hands through his hair in that trait of his that she was coming to know meant he was going to tell her something that was hard for him. He only did that when he was nervous.

"I asked you to come here today because I realized what a fool I'd been. Letting you walk out of my life once was stupid, but twice was completely unacceptable."

"I agree," she said. "What changed your mind?"

He got down on one knee by the couch and reached out to touch the bump of her pregnancy belly. "I don't want our child to grow up the way we did. Shrouded in secrets and living with lies. And that is what will happen unless I tell you something today."

"What?" she asked. "I can't live with a man who doesn't love me."

"I know that and you don't have to. I love you, Nichole."

"Are you sure? A few days ago, you didn't think you could love me."

Conner nodded at her. "I'm very sure. It didn't take me long to figure out that I loved you and that I was afraid to let myself admit it. But not admitting it didn't mean it wasn't true. I've missed you so damn much the last two months. I've thought of nothing but you.

"I love you and I hope that you still love me, but if you don't I'm determined to be the man you need so that I can win your love again."

"I do love you," she said, reaching out to touch his face, then putting her hand over his on her belly. He got to his feet and pulled her into his arms, holding her as close as he could.

"I can't live without you," he whispered in her ear. "I know that you could have an easier life with a man who is more open to emotions, but you won't ever find a man who loves you more than I do."

"I don't want to live without you, either," she said, kissing him solidly.

"Good," he said, going down on one knee again. He pulled a small ring box from his pocket. "Nichole Reynolds, will you do me the honor of being my wife?"

She got down on her knees in front of him and took the ring from him, putting it on her finger. "Yes, Conner, I will be your wife."

Conner hugged her close and then scooped her up and set her on the couch. "I know you're pregnant, but can you have a small sip of champagne to celebrate our engagement?"

"I think one sip will be okay," she said.

"While I open the bottle, why don't you open this?" he asked, handing her another jewelry box.

"You're going to spoil me," she said.

"I think I'm entitled to. I'm the man who loves you, after all," he said.

For a man who'd said he had a hard time admitting to his emotions, now that he had he seemed to be unable to stop.

Nichole was delighted by the charm bracelet and the fireworks charm. "I guess I'm not going to have to crash the party next year?" she asked.

"No, you're going to have unlimited access to my life for all of eternity," he said.

After they toasted their love, Conner carried her into his bedroom where he made love to her. Then he held her in his arms all afternoon while they talked about the future and made love again.

Nichole fell asleep knowing she'd gotten it all: the story of her lifetime with the man of her dreams.

* * * * *

REQUEST YOUR FREE BOOKS!

2 FREE NOVELS PLUS 2 FREE GIFTS!

 Harlequin®

Desire

ALWAYS POWERFUL, PASSIONATE AND PROVOCATIVE

YES! Please send me 2 FREE Harlequin Desire® novels and my 2 FREE gifts (gifts are worth about $10). After receiving them, if I don't wish to receive any more books, I can return the shipping statement marked "cancel." If I don't cancel, I will receive 6 brand-new novels every month and be billed just $4.30 per book in the U.S. or $4.99 per book in Canada. That's a saving of at least 14% off the cover price! It's quite a bargain! Shipping and handling is just 50¢ per book in the U.S. or 75¢ per book in Canada.* I understand that accepting the 2 free books and gifts places me under no obligation to buy anything. I can always return a shipment and cancel at any time. Even if I never buy another book, the two free books and gifts are mine to keep forever.

225/326 HDN FEF3

Name _____ (PLEASE PRINT) _____

Address _____ Apt. #

City _____ State/Prov. _____ Zip/Postal Code

Signature (if under 18, a parent or guardian must sign)

Mail to the **Reader Service:**

IN U.S.A.: P.O. Box 1867, Buffalo, NY 14240-1867
IN CANADA: P.O. Box 609, Fort Erie, Ontario L2A 5X3

Not valid for current subscribers to Harlequin Desire books.

Want to try two free books from another line?
Call 1-800-873-8635 or visit www.ReaderService.com.

* Terms and prices subject to change without notice. Prices do not include applicable taxes. Sales tax applicable in N.Y. Canadian residents will be charged applicable taxes. Offer not valid in Quebec. This offer is limited to one order per household. All orders subject to credit approval. Credit or debit balances in a customer's account(s) may be offset by any other outstanding balance owed by or to the customer. Please allow 4 to 6 weeks for delivery. Offer available while quantities last.

Your Privacy—The Reader Service is committed to protecting your privacy. Our Privacy Policy is available online at www.ReaderService.com or upon request from the Reader Service.

We make a portion of our mailing list available to reputable third parties that offer products we believe may interest you. If you prefer that we not exchange your name with third parties, or if you wish to clarify or modify your communication preferences, please visit us at www.ReaderService.com/consumerschoice or write to us at Reader Service Preference Service, P.O. Box 9062, Buffalo, NY 14269. Include your complete name and address.

HDES11B

Harlequin® Blaze™

red-hot reads

This navy lieutenant is about to get a blast from the past…and start thinking about the future.

Joanne Rock

captivates with another installment of

Men Out of Uniform

Five years ago, photojournalist Stephanie Rosen was kidnapped in a foreign country. Now, with her demons firmly behind her she is ready to move on…and to rev up her sex life! There's only one man she wants, friend and old flame, navy lieutenant Daniel Murphy. Their one night of passion years ago still leaves Stephanie breathless, and with Daniel on leave she's determined to give him a homecoming to remember.

FULL SURRENDER

Available this September wherever books are sold!

Enjoy this sneak peek of USA TODAY *bestselling author*
Maureen Child's newest title
UP CLOSE AND PERSONAL

Available September 2012 from Harlequin® Desire!

"**L**aura, I know you're in there!"

Ronan Connolly pounded on the bright blue front door, then paused to listen. Not a sound from inside the house, though he knew too well that Laura was in there. Hell, he could practically *feel* her standing just on the other side of the damned door.

He glanced at her car parked alongside the house, then glared again at the still-closed front door.

"You won't convince me you're not at home. Your car is parked in the street, Laura."

Her voice came then, muffled but clear. "It's a driveway in America, Ronan. You're not in Ireland, remember?"

"More's the pity." He scrubbed one hand across his face and rolled his eyes in frustration. If they were in Ireland right now, he'd have half the village of Dunley on his side and he'd bloody well get her to open the door.

"I heard that," she said.

Grinding his teeth together, he counted to ten. Then did it a second time. "Whatever the hell you want to call it, Laura, your car is *here* and so are you. Why not open the door and we can talk this out. Together. In private."

"I've got nothing to say to you."

He laughed shortly. That would be a first indeed, he told himself. A more opinionated woman he had never met. He had to admit, he had enjoyed verbally sparring with her. He admired a quick mind and a sharp tongue. He'd admired her even more once he'd gotten her into his bed.

He glanced down at the dozen red roses he held clutched in his right hand and called himself a damned fool for thinking this woman would be swayed by pretty flowers and a smooth speech. Hell, she hadn't even *seen* the flowers yet. At this rate, she never would.

Huffing out an impatient breath, he lowered his voice. "You know why I'm here. Let's get it done and have it over then."

There was a moment's pause, as if she were thinking about what he'd said. Then she spoke up again. "You can't have him."

"What?"

"You heard me."

Ronan narrowed his gaze fiercely on the door as if he could see through the panel to the woman beyond. "Aye, I heard you. Though, I don't believe it. I've come for what's mine, Laura, and I'm not leaving until I have it."

Will Ronan get what he's come for?

Find out in Maureen Child's new title
UP CLOSE AND PERSONAL

Available September 2012 from Harlequin® Desire!

HARLEQUIN®

SytyCW
SO YOU THINK YOU CAN WRITE

Harlequin and Mills & Boon are joining forces in a global search for new authors.

In September 2012 we're launching our biggest contest yet—with the prize of being published by the world's leader in romance fiction!

Look for more information on our website, **www.soyouthinkyoucanwrite.com**

So you think you can write? Show us!